Enemies in Earnest

WILLOW SANDERS

EDITED BY
CRYSTAL GRIZZARD BURNETTE

To my friend, M.A. Foster
Without you, this book would have never gotten finished.
Thank you for being my weekend warrior.

One

WHY WOULD a woman name a bar Temperance? Anyone who speaks with Acacia Ashley for more than two seconds will have zero doubt in their mind that she is probably part alien. No one human could possess that much intelligence.

Acacia Ashley happened to own Temperance, the bar. The very bar I drove past at least four times a day, carting the spring breakers, the midlife crisis cruisers, and the *reliving my glory days* brocationers. What do all of my clients have in common? They're paying me, the proprietor of the *Three Sheets Charters,* for a two-hour trip around the Keys. I ply them with cheap drinks, tell them quippy jokes, and provide dull fodder. So dull that I have to fight against rolling my eyes every time I point to the vapid sign that says "Southernmost point in the U.S." or make the same dippy joke about Santa making a right instead of a left at the equator and deciding to vacation right here in Candy Cane Key.

I hated myself a little more every day for selling out to be a drink slinger and a cheesy joke teller. Sure the money was good. Hell, the money was fucking fantastic. But there had to be more to my existence than twice daily out-and-backs with a bunch of marathon drinkers that I prayed didn't retch over the side of my ship. Especially in front of Acacia's precious bar, lest we re-enact *the incident*.

I think we finally reached a point over the course of the last five years that maybe she was starting to move past it. Back to my original point though. Naming one's bar *Temperance* seems a bit contradictory. The literal definition of temperance is abstinence from drink. It isn't even funnily ironic. It's just strange.

Also, who decides to build a bar on a piece of land surrounded by inlets? Living in the Keys was enough of a hurricane risk already, but then putting a *bar* in a place that was sure to be affected by any kind of swells whether from strong tides or bad weather? Especially someone as neurotic as her. I swear she'd shut up her storm shutters and start battening down the hatches if a gust of wind *sounded* like it was going to bring trouble.

"This drink tastes watered down." Some glory-day-living *bro* in a Hawaiian shirt brought his Mai Tai to where I stood navigating through the inlet.

"Given it is ninety-two degrees today with probably eighty percent humidity, my guess is your ice melted. Just stir it a bit. You'll be fine."

It was just her and some old guy who sat on a stool at the bar. Despite the aforementioned humidity, she wore her long, licorice colored hair down. It practically touched the bow of her sundress while she moved back and forth along the open-air side of her bar.

She had taste. That I would give her. The bar was very

old Havana in a way I wouldn't expect an American who'd never stepped foot in Cuba to understand.

Her patron said something that she found funny. She threw her head back and laughed in what appeared to be a completely genuine way. That was the reason it happened. I'd become so caught up in watching the two of them interact. It was a phenomenon I never witnessed. Whenever I was around, she spit nails, huffed, and generally was one of the orneriest people I ever came in contact with.

Navigating the inlets took finesse. The water was choppy, and the surges from the tide could topple a smaller boat, especially if they weren't experienced. If I had been paying better attention to the idiots on the water, *maybe* it could have been avoided. Some wanna be Captain Ahab out on the high seas with a boat that screamed *overcompensating for something*.

The *"Oh shit! Watch out!"* and various other exclamations of surprise from my clients didn't register in enough time for me to get out of his way. I heard the sickening *clunk* and *crunch* of my boat getting shredded as his monstrosity shoved us into the reef that surrounded Acacia's property. It was a stretch of water I had to traverse every day given my dock was located further down the inlet. I could navigate that passage with my eyes closed.

"I hate when that thousand-year-old coral grows seemingly overnight," she called out from where she washed glasses at her sink. "Stuff kind of jumps out at you, huh?"

"Remind me to never call you as an eyewitness to anything." I pulled out a chair at the closest table and flopped into it. "Since you clearly missed the gigantic fucking boat that crashed into the side of my ship and *pushed* me into your coral, sweetheart."

After dealing with the Coast Guard, ensuring no one needed medical treatment, *thank god*, and getting a ferry to collect the bachelor party and return them to the dock, the last thing I wanted to deal with was her smart assed comments.

"Would it be too much trouble to ask you for a glass of water? Or maybe if you're feeling generous, some iced tea?"

"Tourists." The bearded man seated at the bar huffed into his glass.

Tourists, indeed. The world's most unfortunate double-edged sword. The drivers of our economy in good old Candy Cane Key, and also the cause of never-ending headaches. I was also pretty certain that he, too, fell into that category.

I've lived in Florida all my life. I've owned too many boats to count and sailed the seas since before I had a driver's license. While the jarring, overwhelming Christmas spirit of Candy Cane Key was a bit much for my own personal preferences, my mom had no one else but me, and she'd always dreamed of retiring there.

Was it weird that a forty-two-year-old man lived in a duplex with his mom? Probably. But since Dad passed, knowing I could hear her fall, or any number of emergencies, through the wall, made me feel better about her keeping her autonomy.

"Not to rub salt in the wound," Acacia approached with a basket of peanuts and a glass of sweet tea, that smarmy little tilt to her eyebrow. "But that cigarette boat was a bit hard to miss. What with the sound of a roaring jet plane of an engine and the massive tidal wave of a wake it produces."

The cold condensation on the glass did little to soothe

my grated nerves. Even holding it to my forehead didn't help any. I refused her bait. Even if she dangled her poison from an irresistible iridescent lure.

"Thanks for the tea." I sucked it down in three obnoxious gulps. "But I'll take poking and uncomfortable rocks, and the heat of the midday sun to whatever version of hospitality you're slinging."

I threw down a twenty just to spite her and headed back toward my wreckage of a boat to wait for the hauler to arrive. I guess I was wrong. Forgiveness wasn't part of Acacia's vocabulary. I would have thought after five years we'd be past it, but apparently not.

CHAPTER

Two

Acacia

EDWIN WHEELER WAS the bane of my existence. The *incident* notwithstanding. Even before then he'd been about as enjoyable as a 90s pop song on never-ending repeat. For the past nearly ten years, I'd had to bear witness to his over-the-top theatrics four times a day as he toot-tooted his boat past my bar, packed to the gills with party types that preferred their libations shot from water guns into their gaping maws.

"That wasn't just salt you rubbed into that wound." My customer, Dr. Asher Krane, pulled me out of my musings. "You yanked open that wound and poured Borax into it."

Dr. Asher Krane. Not Asher. Not Dr. Krane. When he introduced himself, it was always *Dr. Asher Krane*. As if the world knew who he was. I did, unfortunately. He'd been my regular patron every day for the last three years. I knew his whole life story. He'd retired from Dartmouth a few years back and decided to live out the rest of his days ala Hemingway. Less the profuse abuse of alcohol.

"If you knew our history, Krane, you would forgive the Borax."

He raised his eyebrow at me over his drink. A Negroni. Because it wasn't pretentious enough to live out one's days as Hemingway would have. But also only drink Hemingway's drinks: a Negroni, a dry martini, or a Highball, depending on the mood.

"Oh yes," he held his hand to his forehead and melted dramatically into the back of his chair. "*The incident.* So cloak and dagger. Veiled in secrecy and otherwise unexcogitable. Cue the *Deus Ex Machina.*"

Whatever word there was *above* pretentious, I think Dr. Asher Krane fit the bill. Half the things he said I had to surreptitiously google on my phone.

"No need for a Shakespearean save, Dr. Krane. That neanderthal with his two buck chuck and his *Mardi Gras*-esque attitude toward business, simply needs to relocate to a section of the harbor that welcomes his sort."

I busied myself with wiping down the bar and handling the orders for the handful of patrons. Despite July being the most active of the tourist months, with *Christmas in July* and *Hemingway Days* drawing various crowds, midafternoon wasn't ever hopping.

"Acacia, you and I have been acquainted for three years now. I've even earned the trust of your ratty old cat. Surely, the fact that I darken the doorstep of this fine establishment nearly every day has earned me a peek into the greatest rivalry on Candy Cane Key. Obviously, I'm a *Capulet* in this case."

Six- toed Joe sat on his perch next to the television, staring impassively at the two of us. He couldn't help his matted looking fur. More than likely, he had some Maine

Coone or Persian in him. Neither long haired breeds were ideal for the heat and humidity of the Keys. Upon hearing his name, Six- toed Joe hopped from his perch and slunk toward Dr. Krane's feet, winding himself around the bar stool.

"See." He picked up the cat, welcoming the head bump. "I don't see him doing this with any of your other patrons."

Dr. Krane, the professor who refused to be addressed by anything other than his formal name, bathed the cat in a lovefest of praise. The man who wore a short-sleeved button-down shirt, tan pants, and bow tie every single day. Who carried beneath his arm, a copy of the local paper and a battered and worn copy of *The Old Man and the Sea*. That man. Mister distinguished professor talked baby talk to my six- toed stray.

"I thought you were a Hemingway expert. What's with all the Shakespearean references today?" I teased.

I took a look around the bar, and seeing everyone was happily engaged in conversations or enthralled with the Marlins game, grabbed a glass of water and leaned against the counter.

"Actually my dear, Hemingway is a passion. Shakespeare paid the bills. And every year around this time, the ennui creeps into the cracks of my soul, and I find myself restless. Desperate. In search of something that will fulfill me in the same way my beloved Shakespeare Festival did. We'd be holding faculty meetings right about now to discuss what the fall production would be. The discourse. Oh, the *discourse!* It's what I miss most. So many like-minded people in one room debating the subtleties of Shakespeare and weighing the positives and negatives of each of his tomes. One of my professors– his name is Dr. Sebastian Doyle. He took over for me, actually, when I left. But he was such a pistol."

It wasn't the first time he'd told me about Dr. Doyle, or his love of Macbeth. It was obvious he loved his job as a professor and literary festival director. "You have so much experience with festivals." I tapped my finger to my lip. "Maybe you can help a damsel in distress with the Hemingway Days celebration? You clearly are an avid fan. I can't think of anyone better suited to be my right-hand man. That is, of course, if you have the time?"

Asher's bushy gray eyebrows shot up so high, the wrinkles on his face flattened. I think it may have been the first time I noticed or was able to see the tawny color of his eyes. I saw the wheels turning. Could practically hear the engine in his brain revving and turning over as he thought about it.

"Hemingway Days are two weeks away. What could you possibly have left to plan?"

Caught me there.

"Well, it's his one hundred and twenty-fifth birthday. That's kind of a big number. It calls for an even bigger celebration, don't you think?"

"A hundred and twenty-five? You don't say. An important milestone, indeed. We'll definitely need to up the ante over your normal reading of his prose and releasing of the wreath into the sea at sunset."

I loved my sunset tribute. Despite *the incident,* that tribute was what I looked forward to every year. There was no more perfect symbolic elegy. Reading about the closing of a chapter, the sunset of one's life, as a symbol of life is released into the sea. It's beautiful and moving.

"I won't give up my sunset tribute."

We'd make that perfectly clear from the onset.

"Come on, Acacia!" One of the other regulars, Julian, called from his table. "The only time that sunset tribute was interesting was the year Edwin's group of cougars flashed their tits at everyone and projectile vomited for the world to witness. Even that hottie novelist, Felix Mercer, reading *Papa's* tomes couldn't up the interest factor."

Asher booped his nose like a 1950s circus clown before shaking his finger at me. It took everything in me not to roll my eyes at him. Gold star to Dr. Krane. Someone told him about *the incident*.

Though it was much worse than that. It wasn't *just* some middle-aged women who couldn't control their drink. No. It was Edwin himself, sucking on a pipe, yucking it up with his clients, telling them to "Come to Papa!" and that he'd take care of them. That happened on the way *out* to sea. Which I'd written off because the celebration hadn't started yet, and it had only been me and a handful of my waitstaff at the time. But then, that asshole had the *audacity* to bring those ladies back to shore right in the middle of my sunset tribute. As if he didn't know we did the exact same thing at seven thirty every year since I'd own the bar. Every year! Like he couldn't have waited ten damn minutes for the wreath to be released.

Those ladies were so hammered they could barely keep themselves standing along the balcony. They'd been so out of their gourd they mistook my twinkle lights for beads. One of them pointed at said twinkle lights screaming, "I'll show you, my tits!" and flashed every somber faced literary great in the area who had come for Hemingway's one hundred and twentieth birthday celebration. Including Hemingway's granddaughter! The woman was so mortified she's never returned a single call or email since.

We used to be her favorite Hemingway bar. She said we were elegant and classy. *"A sophisticated tribute worthy of the esteem of Ernest Hemingway."* Now from what I saw on the internet she visited the *other* Hemingway bar. The one Hemingway *actually* frequented.

"I believe your fans are calling for a recast!" Asher waved his hand in theatrical fashion toward the eleven people seated in the bar.

He pushed out of his chair, gathering his things in the process.

"We start tomorrow!" he shouted and thrust his hand into the air triumphantly. "This will be your comeback year, m'dear."

My comeback? Interesting. If Edwin was the reason for my demise in the first place, why did *I* need a comeback?

WHAT DOES a middle-aged man do when his boat is wrecked and incapacitated for most of the summer tourist season? Play host to cousins, of course. And, taxi his mother around ala *Driving Miss Daisy*. Not that I minded seeing my cousin, Klaus, or meeting his fiancé Felicity.

"Is that a Hemingway bar?" Felicity asked as we drove around the island. "My sister, Sera, would just die. She's a massive book nerd."

"You can come with me this afternoon," my mother offered. "The Candy Cane Key Christmas Society meets there. We're finalizing the Christmas in July activities."

Wasn't that a kick in the Johnson? What a perfect way to spend an afternoon. As if the fact that I was essentially out of business for the near future wasn't depressing enough, I got to sit in Acacia's bar for the next few hours listening to her know it all commentary on my inability to steer a boat.

"We can head down to the wharf while they visit with the coffee clutch," I offered to Klaus. "Listening to the town matriarchs plan their parties probably isn't your idea of a fun vacation."

"Actually," my cousin offered a sheepish smile. "Felicity and I love Christmas. It's what brought us together. The whole reason we picked July to visit was because of the festival."

Of course, it was. Though with a name like *Klaus* a love of Christmas was probably a requirement. The universe hated me. Though I struggled to figure out what, exactly, I'd done to draw its ire.

"MariJo!" Acacia practically skipped toward my mother, all sunshine and smiles, arms spread wide to accept her hug. "I was wondering when I'd see you next. You missed last week's meeting. I was starting to worry."

Acacia was actually quite beautiful. Despite the poison she couldn't resist spitting whenever I was around. She wore her twisted hair in an elegant braid that wrapped around the crown of her head. In place of a dress, she wore a pair of overall shorts and a peach-colored t-shirt with a cockroach on it that read *I Woke Up Like This - Kafka.* Though, I refused to give her the satisfaction of my appreciative chuckle at her punny t-shirt.

However, a man would have to be dead to not be affected by the way she looked. Her lush curves filled out those denim shorts in the most cock-teasing way. And her long, shapely legs highlighted her flawless honey bronze skin.

"Oh, nothing too serious. Just had to go and have some blood drawn. You know how it is with old ladies like me. They find any reason they can to make you a pin cushion and then charge you a hundred dollars for the band aid they fix you up with before sending you on your way."

My mother got smiles and compliments from Acacia. My *mother's* guests that *she* introduced got warm greetings and offers of specials and *on the house* appetizers. And then, Acacia's gaze stuttered over toward me. Her eyes shuttered faster than the town gossip getting caught peeking through her window.

"This is a much tamer clientele than you're used to, Edwin. Would you like me to bring over a tray of shots perhaps? I haven't seen a water gun anywhere, but *maybe* I have some Mardi Gras beads in the back somewhere I can toss your way. What do you say, *Papa*?"

My entire table full of family looked toward me for an explanation. My mom, of course, barely paid attention to anything past her friends and their daily comings and goings. More than likely *the incident* never had been relayed to her.

Rather than linger to hear my response, she sauntered back toward her bar to assemble drinks for another customer.

"Acacia excels in reopening long forgotten, and oft apologized for, wounds."

I waved the topic away with a brusque swipe.

"Is she still mad because of the lady who tossed her cookies over the side of your ship?" my mother asked.

The tossing of the cookies probably would have been forgiven if the other ladies hadn't decided to *shake* theirs. I had no control over the people who booked my charter. If they wanted to get obnoxiously drunk and then pull the little triangles of their string bikini to expose their breasts to the granddaughter of a Poet Laureate, that was *not* my fault.

First I had no idea that Acacia had famous people coming to her little memorial. She hadn't announced that tiny detail to anyone. *Protecting* the family's safety and privacy, she'd said. How was I to know, honestly, that her event would be any different than any of the other ones? Read the passage, drop the wreath in the water, watch the sunset. Rinse, and repeat.

Personally, I chose to remember what it was like before *the incident.* In the magical moments just days before. When the sky glittered with raining fireworks, and boats paraded through the inlet with their Santa themed decorations. The two of us shared a blanket spread out on the grassy knoll between our two harbors. We'd gotten trapped from all the tourists piling *in.* Which prevented us from getting *out* toward the center of town.

We made the best of it. Acacia brought some appetizers that she'd whipped together before the show started. I grabbed a bottle of champagne from the boat's stock. Six-toed Joe sat between us on the blanket entertaining himself with the various winged objects that skittered this way and that. It was the night of possibilities. We were more than two businesspeople who shared a lot line and maintenance bills. That night we very nearly became friends.

Of course, time could be messing with my memories. But perhaps we'd toed the line to *more* than friends. I thought, just as the evening was ending, that there was moment. We collected the debris on the blanket and stood at the same time. She and I were a gasp apart. If I'd leaned in just a millimeter closer, it would have been a kiss. Stupid me. I wanted to be respectful. To consider that we were simply two people making the best out of an annoying evening. I backed off. Pretended I hadn't been about press in to test the feel of her supple, heart-shaped mouth.

"You don't have to stay, you know." My mom patted my

hand, concern lining her face. "I know you have a lot to do. Boat things. If you need to go, just come sometime around five. I think we'll be done by then."

Not a chance. The last time I'd left her to her own devices, one of her planning committee friends, Mrs. Soames, forgot she was supposed to be bringing my mother home and left early with the guy who owned the local hardware store. Thankfully, that meeting had been at the community center and the lovely young thing at the front desk had enough wherewithal to call me to come collect her.

"It's fine Ma. I can keep myself entertained. Besides, it doesn't make sense to go home, and there's nothing for me to do at work without my boat."

Seemingly satisfied, she turned back to Klaus and Felicity, and they regaled us with the story of the snowstorm that brought them together on Christmas Eve. Klaus' mom and my mom were sisters. Aunt Clara and Uncle Ralph starred in some of my favorite memories from childhood, along with Klaus' brother, Leo. As an only child, my mom and dad sent me to Chicago frequently to socialize with *family* so I would have other people to lean on in the unlikely event they left this earth while I was still too young to fend for myself. Always planning for the worst.

But a kid from a sunny state getting to frolic in the snow during Christmas break? I'd looked forward to it. We didn't travel back and forth that frequently. Every three years or so, maybe. But those trips were the highlight of my youth.

"If not for that blizzard, I probably would have spent the rest of my life assuming that there wasn't anyone out there for me." Klaus smiled at his fiancé, taking her hand in his and running his lips along her fingers.

He gave her a look that was both heated and tender. My

chest tightened so fiercely the action choked my airway for the briefest second. There was no way that feeling was *jealousy*. I didn't get jealous. And over a look in his eyes? What was I, a Bronte hero pining for unrequited love?

But there was something that pulsed between them. Not lust, though I certainly didn't miss the way Felicity's pupils expanded. It was different. All encompassing. I wanted to look down into someone's eyes and see that.

Like that didn't hit me like a two by four. Me, suddenly pining for love? The only love I'd ever had was the sea. Exactly how it should be. Yet—something barely discernible whispered in my ear. Desperate for something *more*.

"I think we need some champagne. It's not every day that one of my oldest childhood friends gets engaged *and* comes to visit. Mom, are you going to join in the toast?"

Technically, she shouldn't be drinking. Drug interactions. But it was a special occasion and honestly a little touch to her lips was probably as much *drinking* as she'd do. Though given I'd have to face Her Highness, Queen of Smart Assed Comments and Opinionated Commentary, having my mother's consent was my shield for placing my order and collecting the spirits unscathed.

Acacia

IT WAS MUCH EASIER to ruminate over one's nemesis when he wasn't ten feet away. The other problem? The way he doted on and cared for his mother was literally catnip. Lady Kitty catnip, not like, for Six-toed Joe. The second his mom shivered, he was there with her cardigan. She coughed, he had her water at the ready. He repeated what MariJo's nephew and niece said, but louder and in the direction of her good ear, without making it obvious he did it for her benefit. How could someone who was such an *asshole* be so sweetly attentive to his mother? It didn't compute.

"What if we served a buffet of Hemingway inspired appetizers?" Asher asked, his bushy eyebrows the only thing I could make out over the clipboard he referenced.

"Now wouldn't that be a hoot." Edwin flipped a fifty onto the counter. "I'm sure no one in the history of Hemingway inspired bars, restaurants, parties, or events has ever thought to offer a little canapé dipped in literary puns."

Asher lifted an eyebrow in his direction as if to ask me *is he for real?* Unfortunately, yes, he was. The two of us had a *War and Peace* length conversation in silent eye-rolls and quirks of lip before Asher heaved a dramatic sigh and placed his clipboard on the counter.

"I believe it was the great Oscar Wilde who said *sarcasm is the lowest form of wit.*"

Edwin nabbed a cherry from my garnish center, shrugging in Asher's direction. God, he was ridiculous. He never took his eyes off me, even though the shrug was directed at Asher. Did he want me to chastise him for stealing a cherry? Because of the list of things I could chastise the man over, being a cherry stealer was low on the list.

"What can I do for you Edwin?"

I tried to be as subtle as I could, affixing the plastic top to the tray of garnish. It was a place of business after all. Sanitation was important. Certainly no one wanted his grubby, work roughened fingers anywhere near their drinks.

"Now there's a statement heavy with possibility."

Edwin Wheeler did not get to do funny things to my nervous system. No ma'am. The way his voice went soft and gravely did *not* affect the steady, reliable thrum of my pulse. And his tipped lip or the mischievous glint in his eyes did not make my face feel hot. I'd rather succumb to food poisoning from bad fish than have *him* be the reason I felt flushed and a little woozy.

"Did your mom call up your cousin and ask him to come for a playdate? That was so considerate of her. This way you have someone who is obligated to tolerate your company every day while your boat's boo-boos get all patched up."

At that moment, the sexy version of Santa Claus, also

known as Edwin's cousin, took a seat next to him at the bar and regarded me.

"How's that champagne coming along?" he asked his cousin.

"This here's Klaus." Edwin cocked his head.

"Bottle or glasses?" I asked, ignoring the flirty challenge in Edwin's eyes. "The bottle is probably the better choice as you'll get four glasses out of it for thirty dollars versus four glasses of champagne at nine fifty a piece which would be thirty-eight, before tax."

Edwin's eyes flit to the fifty he had sitting in front of him and back up to look at me. Though that didn't really answer the question. Regardless of which he chose, the fifty covered it and then some.

He didn't get to win. It was my bar. If I were a petty person, I'd pour four glasses and charge him the per glass rate. If he wanted to play Mr. Unaffected, James Dean cool, and answer me in smirks and eyebrow lifts instead of words, fine. I'd show him.

But his boat did just get totally decimated by a cigarette boat. Even if his insurance covered the accident, he wouldn't recoup his income from the rest of his season. It was entirely possible that he threw the fifty down to save face with his cousin, but that unspoken eyebrow lift said something like *I'll come back for that when he's not paying attention.*

"On the house, gentlemen."

I put the bottle in the middle of a tray, four glasses surrounding it. Klaus nodded his thanks at me, taking the tray and carrying it to the table. Edwin, on the other hand, appeared cemented in place.

"Your charity isn't necessary."

He tapped the fifty still sitting on the bar and pushed it closer to where my hands rested.

"Not charity. Just adding to the excitement of the celebration. Look how happy your mom looks. If nothing else, her smile is worth more than President Grant's face can pay me."

I saw the storm brew in his eyes. A gale force collecting in the horizon threatening to come to shore. Just like the anticipation of a thunderstorm, the hair on my arms began to rise in reaction to the pouty set of his mouth and his cocked head.

I thought for sure he was about to make some kind of snarky comment. He just... turned around! He left the fifty on the bar, turned around, and walked back toward the table without another word. The nerve.

"Can you believe that?" I huffed in Asher's direction.

"That you castrated his pride right in front of his cousin? I am a bit surprised, yes."

Not the supportive commentary I expected from my octogenarian side kick.

"Or that I tried to be nice and give him a free bottle of champagne for their celebration and he pretty much gave me the finger? That's what it looked like from where I'm standing."

Asher set the clipboard down on the bar as if it were a sleeping infant he'd just rocked to sleep after hours of colic. He cast a look toward Edwin's table while apparently considering what to say. I followed his gaze, watching the banter between Edwin and his cousin. Klaus apparently had said something that had Edwin in stitches, covering his eyes as his whole body curled with laughter.

With the members of the Christmas Society beginning

to roll in, the ambient noise had increased significantly. I couldn't hear a word of their conversation. Watching Edwin in side-grabbing hysterics, though, was a sight I'd never seen from the old sourpuss.

"You spent the last thirty minutes needling him, and then graciously comp his drinks. It's either pity or charity to make yourself look good to others. Either way, not a good look for you, dear."

EVEN THOUGH KLAUS and Felicity had planned to visit well before the incident with my boat, there couldn't have been a more perfect time for them to come.

"Do you remember Astrid Schneider?" Klaus knocked his shoulder against mine while we listened to the Christmas planning committee drone on about the upcoming festivities.

"Name rings a bell," I rubbed my forehead trying to knock the dusty filing cabinets in my brain around to find where that name existed.

"She went to school with Leo and I," Klaus prodded. "You were her date to Rosenball. It was the year Leo's friend, Charlie, pilfered some Gluhwein, and we spent the evening on the gym mats in the community center supply closet."

He raised his eyebrows at me as if that detail alone should bring this whole memory careening back to my consciousness.

"Those details don't matter. She's in New York now.

Felicity and I recently ran into her at this charity thing. She's a newscaster."

"Are we talking about Astrid?" Felicity joined in, smiling at Klaus. "She was the one who taught Klaus how to umm…"

Felicity blushed as pink as the t-shirt she wore. She looked over her shoulder at my mom, who was intently listening to the discussion of the upcoming boat parade. When she was sure my mom wasn't looking at her, she spread two of her fingers wide and stuck her tongue between them in the universal signal for licking the kitty.

I damn near spit my drink out in a glorious shower of cheap champagne.

"Of all the things I expected to witness from your fiancé this week, *that* was not one of them."

I tried valiantly to keep my hysterics to myself. Not wanting to disrupt the meeting in progress or draw the attention of the sassy mouth in the punny t-shirt tending the bar. I already had enough beef with her to make a week's worth of lunches.

"She still remembers you fondly," Klaus continued, attempting to hold back his own laughter.

"I guess you're really great at following directions." Felicity giggled around a sip of champagne. "Some may even say, exceptional."

"I should send her a thank you basket." I continued, only adding fuel to the hysterics pile. "Complaint free for twenty-three."

I raised my glass in mock toast, hardly expecting the pair to actually toast me. Which had us splintering into more laughter. There were enough people in the bar that it was loud enough for our table talk to barely register over the chatter. Add to it the microphone from my mom's planning committee and the ambient noise dialed up to ear splitting.

"Actually!" My mom raised her hand and stood, trying to signal Wanelda. "I think my nephew, Klaus, should be this year's Santa. Look at him! He'd have all the ladies drooling!"

Dozens of details converged simultaneously. None of them less important than any other, but my mother whoring out my beefcake cousin to *make the ladies drool* was not something I would have expected from my frail, always cold, nearly eighty-year old mother. In front of his fiancé no less.

"Um, mom. Did you forget that *I'm* Santa for the boat parade?" I asked, honestly stunned that I would be pushed out of the way with little preamble. Even if Klaus was my cousin. The *sexy Santa* commentary hadn't escaped my notice, either. Still. Since old man Withersby stepped down five years ago, I was the town Santa.

"You don't even have a boat right now, Eddie," she said. "And besides, a little eye candy will help keep the tourists here for a little longer. And that is good for all of us."

Eye candy. From my mother's mouth. My nearly eighty-year-old mother was slinging sex to draw in tourists. Clearly that crash with Mr. Big Boat rattled my brain or hit me clear into an alternate universe. My sweet mother, the one who knits blankets for Harlow's strays and buys season tickets to the playhouse she rarely attends, had been replaced by one winking and licking her finger, pressing it against her hip while she made sizzling noises. The bleating hens of her group egged her on further by clapping and hooting. Jesus, I needed a drink. Bearing witness to all of this was causing a rip in the space/time continuum. Any minute I expected to be yanked out of the bar and dropped into my actual reality.

"I'd like a beer, please. Hefeweizen if you have it. If not, whatever wheat ale you have."

Acacia regarded me for a long moment. I saw something ticking behind the deep indigo hue of her eyes. For a second it almost looked like she was going to say something nice. She licked those sensuous lips of hers, her mouth relaxed in a sheepish smile.

But rather than say whatever was on her mind, she busied herself with the beer fridge behind her. Bent at the waist, sorting through the various bottles displayed on those shelves, any normal human being would focus their attention on the baseball game on the television, or the gorgeous horizon just beyond where we sat. Me? I couldn't take my eyes off her luscious peach of an ass pressing against the denim of her overalls. With her leaned over as she was, the cuff of those shorts creeped up to reveal just the beginning hints of her satin panties. She was not a thong girl. Which didn't surprise me in the slightest. To be honest, I thought for sure she'd be a boring, white cotton, granny panty kind of gal. Instead, I was surprised to see what appeared to be a pair of gray satin cheeky panties based on how well they were lifting and separating her derriere.

"You may want to slow down there, partner." She placed the beer in front of me with a wink. "That's two whole drinks you've consumed in my bar. I think you're about to set a record for length of time spent in this establishment."

"Surely you saw my mother stand and shimmy her hips and use words like *eye candy*."

I studied her like a kid cramming for a surprise exam. I watched her eyes leave mine, flit over my shoulder and land in the general direction from where I'd just come. Her lips tipped into a smile, and her nose did this cute wrinkle I assumed when she spotted my mom.

"Aw, she's having fun. She really looks forward to this time with the ladies."

"That reminds me, why exactly *is* this meeting being held here?"

"Because I'm on the planning committee?" Her voice went up at the end in question, as if any moron knew that.

Figures.

"Well, planning committee member, perhaps you heard that I've been stripped of my duties for the holiday light boat show. Apparently, the ladies want the newer, sleeker version."

I toss my head in Klaus' direction. Presently, he flexed for one of the fawning women who'd taken hold of his arm. Obviously he was super uncomfortable with all the attention. Just then, he stood, raised his t-shirt just slightly to give all the biddies a little show of his well-defined abs. Even his fiancé was egging him on tossing dollars at his feet.

"Aww, poor Faulkner."

Acacia tilted her head, her voice dripping with mock sympathy. Her barfly friend, Dr. Asher Krane, still sat perched where he always was, sipping his Negroni. At Acacia's esoteric comment, Krane chortled into his drink.

"I'm sorry?" I asked, looking toward Krane, since I was sure Acacia would not bother to enlighten me.

"Oh, come now, son. The notorious rivalry between Hemingway and Faulkner? Surely someone who lives on this island and slings trivia all day long to the tourists knows even the most basic information about its most famous resident."

That was a no. I knew the bare minimum. I'd read a few of his books. Not saying they weren't decent. Guy could tell a good tale. But I wasn't Acacia. I didn't fawn and faint over every fork he touched or tree he pissed on.

"What did they teach you at Party U?" Acacia pointed to my Florida Gators t-shirt. "Beer pong? Hangover remedies? How to stack your parties to keep the best buzz going?"

I realized at that moment while I searched for a comeback, there was little I knew about Acacia. She bought the bar about ten years ago. That I knew. Her father was a famous entomologist who studied rare bugs that only existed in the Keys. Her mom and dad lived up north, near Destin. But we rarely had any kind of conversations where we learned about one another. Most of our conversations were about taxes, the cost of that month's utilities, and commentary on the success or lack of from the different pitches and yaw of the tourist season. One would assume based on her obnoxious little dig, that her educational pursuits must have been higher reaching than that of a state university.

"No state colleges for you then, I assume. And what apex of educational pursuits did you deign to attend?"

Dr. Asher Krane failed at his attempt to hide his surprised chortle. Rather than reply, Acacia chose to busy herself with wiping down the bar and ensuring all of her glasses aligned just so in the holster above her head. It didn't matter to me. Her attempted dig at my intellect was reaching at best. That's what I told myself, anyway.

Just because I was out of work, and now not even the preferred choice for the city's Santa Claus, meant nothing in the grand scheme of things. I was a successful business owner. Not having a boat was a minor setback. My boat would be back in no time.

Acacia

MAYBE I TOOK our banter too far. I wasn't exactly the queen of undeterrable confidence and witty repartee. My experience with banter came in the form of a handsome hunk of a man in the latest romcom I streamed from my living room while eating gelato. Or the swoony, heartrending romance of the varied literary eras. My own romance? That well was so dry, my body submitted a rezoning permit to Death Valley. Because that was about as likely as finding a man in Candy Cane Key. Or any of the keys really. Hell, I'd even settle for a commute to Miami.

The Miami men were too urbane. They wanted collagen and six-inch fuck me heels, and nights spent being seen at the trendiest club. All of which sounded as pleasant as being covered in honey and eaten by fire ants.

The Keys men were...well, they just lacked something. Not to group them all together, but each man I'd taken interest in was too much of something or not enough of another. I never thought I was a picky person. I didn't think my requirements were too much. Well read, and it didn't even matter *what* they read. Military history, sci fi, popular fiction—just so that they were experiencing something from the written word. This desire seemed to be the crux of every single potential suitor I'd found. No one reads anymore.

Maybe that was why I found Asher's company so pleasant. He always had an observation or discussion at the ready on any number of books from the literary greats to the most recent thriller. Unfortunately, a nearly forty-year age gap wasn't really my thing.

But I'd been on Candy Cane Key for nearly ten years. In the beginning, I thought maybe Edwin and I could be a thing. We were closer together in age. Before *the incident* he'd been able to hold up his end of a conversation at any number of community gatherings.

And then there was this one time when I'd gotten so absorbed in my plans for Hemingway Day that I'd lost track of time. It was the day of the boat parade, back when Old Man Withersby was still our Santa, and all of the traffic down to the marina boxed me in and cemented me in place. The day had been shit. I just wanted to go home and soak in the bathtub with a glass of wine and an audiobook.

Edwin saw the light on in the bar. I'm ninety percent certain he'd intended to participate in the boat parade that night. The outfit he'd been in looked like the beginning of a pirate's costume. Though he said he'd gotten stuck by the influx of visitors, as well. He brought some blankets from his boat and set them out on this sad little patch of grass we had between the property lines along with some champagne and a bag of Twizzlers.

Not to be outdone, I grabbed some of my easier to prepare appetizers and we created a mini picnic right there on our little grassy knoll. It was just a boat parade and fireworks. Nothing spectacular. But for those few magical hours, we felt like *something*. Sure we hadn't the kind of intense, cerebral conversations that I had with Dr. Krane, but the conversation never lagged or stuttered. I had *fun*. At the end of the night after the last firework popped and the cheering from the banks died down, Edwin helped me to my feet, and I swear there had been a moment. It happened so fast that over the years I've nearly convinced myself it never happened. That I've created it in my head. But I swear, he wanted to kiss me. Our mouths were so close. If I'd just leaned in, or looked up at him, or bit my lip—any of the things the girls do in the movies when they want a guy to know they'd totally be down for a lip lock. But I am not the kind of person that does well with subtle cues.

Just like the line I'd just crossed. Apparently. My body goes haywire when he's around. And I'm stuck in this vortex of not being able to think straight, hating the way my libido responds to his attention—regardless of the attention—and also wanting to knock myself upside the head. Especially because of the incident. Most certainly because of his piggish behavior. What kind of man encourages women to flip open their bathing suit tops to flash passersby? And what kind of woman still finds that man ridiculously attractive even after he yelled *Come to Papa* and doused them all with a Super Soaker water gun?

"You look like you've been sucking on a lemon for the last half hour." Asher pulled me from my ruminations.

While the rest of the discussions surrounding the next week's festivities, he and I had also been working on the *new and improved* Hemingway Day tribute. All of our resident writers would partake. We asked them to both share their favorite Hemingway tomes, as well as provide meditation on its symbolism and meaning to them personally. The kind of stuff that literary types loved. Asher had made a good point. People who travel down here to be near Hemingway did so because they were voracious consumers of literature. They wanted to be immersed in it. And that included engaging in discourse with other readers and writers.

Once the day was completed, all of the writers and our guests would read the passage from *The Old Man and the Sea* together while I placed the wreath. Pure poetry. While I never expected Asher to both accept the task and buy into my celebration, working with him so far had been a dream.

"I feel bad." I admitted. "I was trying to be funny and banter-y. People in these parts take pot shots at the universities all day. I went to Oxford though! It's not the same over there! I don't know what the rules are for insulting each other's schools."

I could feel my core temperature dialing up to the fires *of Mordor*. My panic was a freight train bearing down on me with broken brakes and a bridge that sported a gaping hole in the middle of the tracks. Asher's cool hand on my own helped pull me back from the edge of total panic. The cold bottle of water he placed in my hand provided even more relief.

"Have you ever thought of asking him to dinner and just hashing this out? Not just the incident but all this sexual tension that crackles every time the two of you are within ten feet of one another."

He was out of his gourd. Sure *my* libido produced enough energy for the both of us. But him? I felt nothing but an arctic chill.

"While his mom is chatting it up with Lady Frost and Wanelda Albright, why not go find Edwin and ask him to dinner. Give him *parlay*. Agree to lay down your figurative weapons and meet to broker negotiations of a truce."

A truce. That was a great idea. Maybe if the two of us could just sit down and talk we'd realize all of this petty back and forth was beneath us.

The dinner rush was in its early stages. Groups stood in the waiting area while the planning committee vacated their tables and the waitstaff turned them. Where the bar had been a sleepy old gin joint a few hours ago, it now pulsed with a rush of people. I had no idea where Edwin had gone. I spotted his cousin and fiancee out on the patio, taking pictures of them with the afternoon hazy sun behind them. His mom still chatted with the rest of the planning committee, though they'd moved over to a corner so as not to hog any of the tables. Every time I caught a Gators t-shirt out of the corner of my eye, I thought it was him but Jesus, the whole word apparently went to the University of Florida.

I'd given up and turned to head back to the bar to make sure my team had accurate coverage when I smacked right into the sappy, smiley gator on the very t-shirt I'd been looking for. A tidal wave of details smacked into me simultaneously. First, Edwin's chest was *hard*. Working on a boat heaving those anchor lines made whatever body he hid under that shirt deliciously chiseled. Second, someone who worked on a boat slinging one-liners for tourists should smell like exhaust or seaweed. Not the perfect combination of dryer sheets and an ocean breeze. I wanted to bury my face in his scent. Third, his strong arms felt like heaven wrapped around my body. Strong arms that continued to hold me long after I bounced off that chiseled marble he called a chest.

"Sorry," I blurted, as I realized who stood in front of me.

"Shit. Ugh. Sorry." I continued to fumble after realizing *who* it was and because I said *shit* and I didn't want him to think I thought he was a piece of shit.

He didn't let go. Just looked at me, his eyes rapidly moving back and forth to catch my gaze. The man could be a world class poker player. Not a single emotion flitted across that face as we stood there.

"I was looking for you actually." I cleared my throat and stepped back in an attempt to create some distance.

That weird zinging thing started happening again. I felt the electric current that hummed between us from my fingertips all the way up and down my spinal cord. Even the hair on my arms and on the back of my neck rose in response to whatever gathered strength like a tidal wave.

"Me? What could you possibly insult now? You've insulted my intellect, my common sense, my ability to run a successful business, and the ability to make friends. The only thing you haven't insulted is my manhood, and I promise you, little seedling, any insulting commentary could easily be proven wrong in a second flat."

It took more than a second for that tiny detail and its implication to disperse to all of the thinking parts of my brain. And even then, I had zero response. What could I possibly say? Congrats? Prove it? Because I was not opposed to him proving it to be honest. The guy walked around in board shorts, Hawaiian shirts and flip flops. A wardrobe like that didn't give much away.

"... it's actually kind of ironic."

I missed something. That's what I got thinking about what kind of banana was swinging in the mesh hammock of his board shorts. Of course, looking at him probably was also a mistake. Because rather than look pissed, flummoxed, or any negative emotion, those cerulean colored orbs looked wild. As if he hadn't eaten for months and someone set a steak down in front of him. He looked like an apex predator circling his prey.

"What is?"

I shouldn't have taken the bait. No matter the timbre of his voice, or the quirky smile on his lips, or how fantastic he smelled…it was a trick. A shiny lure to bait me into chomping down on his hook.

He stood too close. The nearness of his body to mine had already set my body on overdrive and that was before he took another step. He eviscerated my personal space. Backed me clear up against the wall that led to the bathroom, and then took another half step. I could feel the suggestion of his stubble against my cheek as he leaned in to whisper in my ear. My body, a whirring, uncontrollable tornado of sensation couldn't figure out if it wanted to be agitated that he invaded my personal space or delighted with the way his presence teased at my nervous system.

"The way you hide behind your pretentious, erudite trivialities but have missed the giant billboard that shouts from the rafters that you and I are *exactly* the same, Sweet Acacia."

I know words like pretentious were not compliments. His words though, regardless of the barb that was wrapped in them, were delivered in a lullaby soft voice that had me leaning into his mouth to luxuriate in the way his voice vibrated straight down my spinal cord. I wanted to push back. To tell him what a jackass he was, or at minimum, get some space between the two of us. I was hanging limp on his hook, slowly being reeled in toward the eminent death of my pride. My brain could have been a naval landing strip with as many flags it waved, yet my body was drunk on the heady, sexual promise of his voice.

"And how is that?"

That was not what I intended to say. And it definitely was supposed to be delivered with enough heat to get him to back off and call uncle. Instead, he advanced the final few inches so he pressed up against my body fully. At least, that's what I thought he'd done. The moment he did my core temperature raised so high I practically felt my ovaries popping out eggs like gumballs.

"You can hide behind your fancy Hemingway bar and quote his prose."

His fingers felt like clouds against my forehead. I wouldn't have thought someone with such rough hands could be so tender. Every wisp of hair he cleared from my face coiled the desire that flamed hot in my belly even tighter.

"But in the end, Sweet Acacia..."

He pressed his lips to my forehead. They were warm and soft, the perfect kissing lips. And I *wanted* that kiss. I wanted more kisses. A night of them where we collapsed in a breathless heap on a blanket beneath the fireworks.

"The simple fact remains that we are both just drink slingers for tourists."

His words hung in the air. As if they floated on clouds in front of us. It was as if I could see and read the words, but it stopped there. They didn't sink in. I couldn't formulate any understanding beyond the feathery soft brush of his hair against the top of my forehead, his fingers caressing my cheek, that warm press of his lips, and the oceany scent of *him*.

I felt my fingers latch on to his t-shirt, like if I didn't grab him for purchase I'd get sucked into a vortex and deposited in an alternate reality. Beneath my fingertips his skin felt warm...and *firm*. My body froze beneath his gaze. His heated interest slid along my skin, leaving a trail of gooseflesh in its path.

As quick as a clap of thunder, his lips were on mine. Or mine were on his. I have no idea who started kissing whom. But that kiss was heaven and hell. Sin and salvation. It felt like we kissed for hours in the span of a millisecond. I felt every swipe of tongue and press of lip. I swear I heard every grumble and moan working its way up his throat. And then, as fast as that tempest swelled, it dissipated.

"Dinner?"

It was the only word that came to mind. Plenty of expressions floated in that whirlpool, but I feared speaking half of them since they were some phrase or another for *please let's go back to my apartment and satisfy this ache from my gumball ovaries and clenching uterus.*

"Come again?" he asked.

"Ummm...." That wasn't what I'd expected. "Dinner?" I asked again, my voice going up in that weird sing-song way. "Not tonight if you have plans... you know because your family is here and of course, you probably have plans because why wouldn't you have plans with your family that probably flew thousands of miles to come and see you. But maybe...at some point... we could go and have dinner... together. I really like Nicko's. They have Greek food? But if you don't like Greek food there's like, you know, burgers and stuff, too."

He tilted his head, looking at me as if I were a little baby kitten with a tiny fluff ball from the dryer that was going to town as if it were the most entertaining toy they'd ever had the pleasure to play with. I could almost hear him thinking *aww, she's so precious.* But not in a good way.

"Okay. Well. I have to get back to the bar. So, this was great." I signaled between the two of us feeling absolutely moronic. "I guess I'll see you around sometime."

I did a double-barreled finger point. Like I was shooting my *I'm too cool* vibe out the tips of my fingers. No need to combust from the heat of a kiss when the drenching, cold shame of being eternally awkward promised a much slower, and more dramatic, death.

I slid out from underneath his very muscular body that still pressed me against the wall by the bathrooms. The cold showers worth of embarrassment dousing my body shocked me into beelining for the safety of my bar. Except I couldn't move. I tried, but my body stayed firmly in place.

"When?" he asked.

I realized his hand was on my bicep. His strong, warm hand that had moments ago brushed little baby flyaways from my forehead.

"Tomorrow?" I asked.

"What time do you get off?"

I wanted to say something flirty or sassy. But I was not a flirty or sassy person. That was well established.

"Anytime you want me."

Not exactly the flirty I hoped for. Weird? Absolutely. Pathetic show of my lack of game? A thousand percent. He smirked at me.

"How about six o'clock. Do you think Taffy can cover dinner on her own?"

Taffy was my back of house manager. She took care of everything pertaining to my cooks and servers. I wanted to tell him how awesome she was. How capable and smart, that she ran circles around his ass and the one guy named Skeeter that worked his booking desk. Instead, I just nodded.

"Dinner should be interesting," he rumbled, finally releasing my arm. "I'll see you then, Sweet Acacia."

THERE WERE EASILY a million reasons why kissing Acacia had been a gigantic mistake. Going to dinner with her? A monumental lapse in judgment. That's why Klaus and Felicity were being forced to come too. Sad that a forty-two-year-old man needed a babysitter, but I feared what I would do in Acacia's presence.

That kiss knocked me on my ass. Figuratively, of course. I couldn't stop thinking about it. Not on my drive home. Not while sitting on the back porch playing cards, or while my mom and Felicity chatted about the upcoming *Christmas in July* festivities. Even listening to them laugh and gush over Klaus and the *Sinful Santa* they wanted him to be— dressed in tight candy cane striped bike shorts and all –for the parade couldn't dampen my spirits.

The only way that kiss could have been more perfect is if it had happened five years ago, seated on that blanket, while we watched the fireworks. But that's what happens when you don't sack up. You miss a perfect opportunity and spend years regretting it.

"Tell me again why we're here?" Klaus looked out the window of my truck, eyeing Nick's like someone was going to walk out of the front door and douse him in Christmas sprinkles.

"Just in case I need an easy exit. Wait here until I text you. Then, just get a booth, have dinner on me, enjoy all the Christmas kitsch, and watch for a follow up text. If I say I need help, you just need to come and pretend to bump into us. I'll find a way to escape," I told him.

I don't tell him the real reason I need a babysitter. Just in case that same magnetic pull reared its ugly head again—I wanted a stop gap so I didn't suggest she come back to my place. As badly as I wanted to spread her out and spend hours worshipping her, it was a very bad idea. Very bad. Especially with thin walls and guests on the other side of the duplex.

Well, and the fact that she hated me. Hate fucking is always a bad idea. We couldn't get embroiled in any kind of dalliance. Not when we brought the worst out in each other. It would just end in broken hearts, and then we'd become the *Luke and Lorelei* of Candy Cane Key. Suddenly the whole town would be sporting blue and pink ribbons.

Nicko's wouldn't have been on my radar for places Little Miss Prim and Proper patronized. Though she'd surprised me with the whole *I'm on the planning committee* nonsense. I never would have pegged her for one of the Christmas *cookies*. The ones who leaned hard into the Christmas theme of the island.

I saw her from the window in the door. She stood, laughing with the hostess, her head thrown back in complete unguarded delight. It took my breath away. Not just how completely unguarded she was in her laughter, but she'd dressed for the occasion, and she looked... *stunning.*

While the dress was by no means immodest, it did something for her figure. Acacia put hourglass figures to shame. She was the thrill of a winding mountain in a sportscar that turned like it was on rails.

My hands tingled with the remembrance of how that body felt the day prior. Even with the bulk of her overalls she'd been soft in every place I worshipped—like her hips, ass, and thighs– and firm in places that begged for my mouth to tease and touch, like the breasts that pressed against my chest as we kissed.

"Acacia." I placed a chaste kiss on her cheek. "You are an absolute vision."

I assumed she'd gotten dressed up for me. Maybe that was a dickish thing to assume. But the dinner had implications of being a *date* and when her hair was curled in soft rings that seductively cupped her breasts and her makeup did that swoopy thing along her eyes to make them more feline...it felt like she'd done it for me.

"You owe me an apology," she said by way of greeting, pressing a red lacquered fingertip into my chest.

It took me a minute to recover. I'd expected a returned kiss. A smile. Some kind of show of affection that hinted she felt the pull as much as I had. That she had been powerless to it too. And, despite me telling Klaus he was a babysitter to ensure I didn't do anything wrong, I also wanted the satisfaction of knowing I wasn't the only one that hadn't stopped thinking about it since last night.

"An apology?" I asked just as the hostess stepped out from behind her podium with two menus.

"And will you be sitting in the nice or the naughty section tonight?" she asked.

"This one is *definitely* naughty," I told the hostess. "Sit us in the *so naughty Santa's calling Krampus* section."

The heat seeking missiles Acacia called eyeballs bore into my profile as we followed *Hannah,* according to her nametag.

"I should storm out of here right now and make you eat by yourself!" she hissed at me as we wound through the restaurant, past the Christmas karaoke. Thank god being naughty meant you didn't get placed in that version of Chinese Water Torture. I liked my ear drums intact, thank you very much.

"You're the one that invited me to the dinner, or did you forget in all that sexual haze?"

I pulled out her chair when Hannah finally stopped at a table, thankfully tucked in the back corner. Acacia looked at me like I had two heads. She stared down at me over the tip of her nose, her proud chin jutted in defiance.

"Sit, Acacia."

"Oh, first I'm pretentious. Then I'm nothing more than a beer wench. And now I'm an animal you can bring to heel with a cluck of your tongue and a pat of your leg? I think not." She huffed, crossing her arms and tapping her toe.

"I called you pretentious before we kissed, Acacia. Wouldn't the time to be upset about that have occurred prior to the kiss and the dinner invitation?"

Even angry and a little flummoxed, she still stood proud. Like Joan of Arc or some other super feminist warrior that I knew shit all about. I had to remind myself—again—that this dinner couldn't be anything more than clearing the air. Because hate fucking was a terrible, terrible idea. And Acacia made it loud and damn clear I was beneath her. Less than beneath her. A cockroach was higher on the ladder than I was.

"Look." I folded my hands in front of me, staring at her dead in the eyes. "I don't know why, today, you're upset, but I'm sorry. I don't want to fight with you. When you take jabs at my college and my intellect, however, it does toe you into the bullseye of pretentiousness. If you don't like the word, don't judge people based on assumptions."

She didn't budge. Figures. Why would anything with Acacia Ashley be easy? "Where *did* you go to school anyway?"

"Oxford," she said. "My dad went there. He wanted me to go there too."

Pretentious to the nth degree. But I kept that judgment in my head.

"Why don't you sit down and tell me about Oxford. How did your dad end up there?"

She wavered. It was barely a centimeter, but I saw her body flinch like she wanted to sit down. But as soon as the delight fluttered across her features, it was gone again. Jesus, she was exhausting.

"Acacia, might I remind you, again, that *you* invited *me* to dinner. So we can continue to play this tiresome game of you stubbornly holding on to this self-righteous offense or we can just pull out our white flags and call a truce to whatever it is that has made you hate me for the last five years."

The emotions that played across her face rivaled a vaudevillian. I watched with rapt attention as the offense registered first—because how dare I call her stubborn when that was exactly how she was acting. Then the lightbulb went on, that oh *yeah! I* was in fact the guest and she, the host. And she was a shitty host.

"I heard someone has been *very naughty* over here." A holiday elf approached the table, feigned reproach looking foreign on his cheery, glitter coated cheeks.

I take back what I said earlier about how much I hated having to schlep tourists around and crack cheesy jokes that made me die inside. Wearing an elf costume, as a graying, forty-year-old man and talking in a dippy voice, would be the acme of torture by tourism.

"Oh yes, Santa definitely needs to know." I told him, mimicking his syrupy, over the top theatrics. "Acacia should definitely be taken over Santa's lap and given a good spanking."

Her eyebrows shot to her hairline before dropping and furrowing into the sharpest frown lines I had witnessed on anyone younger than eighty.

"This is not that kind of establishment, Wheeler." The man, whose name tag identified him as *Yiannis,* unloaded two drinks called *Gettin' Figgy With It.* "Here's some naughty drinks for the two of you."

Neither of us had even placed a drink order. Also, I had no idea who Yiannis was or how he knew my name given I tended to avoid the popular local places. I guess my reputation preceded me.

Once he left, I took a hearty sip of the Figgy *Christmas on Crack*—way too sweet for my personal liking or someone who didn't want to send my glucose levels into full nuclear panic—and started again.

"You know exactly why I have very strong feelings for you."

She spat the words. I know they were supposed to be

heated and full of rage, but what she said yanked a full bellied laugh from me.

"Oh, do you now? I'm flattered."

The flush went clear up to the tips of her ears.

"You *ruined* Hemingway Day. On his *one hundred and twenty-birthday,* no less. Do you know we had his *family* there, Mr. 'Show Me Your Tits!'"

"I never said 'Show Me Your Tits!' Last I checked we're not on Bourbon Street, sweets. And I have absolutely no control over who comes into my boat or how much they choose to drink. It's a *booze cruise.* They're in the Keys to party. I provide the party. Would you deny me my right as an American business owner to deliver stellar service that at minimum *meets* expectations?"

I'd never seen Acacia slam a drink. Hell, most of the time she was sipping on sophisticated wines from special glasses in varying sizes while discussing *bouquets* and *noses.* But she cleared that sugar coma *naughty* drink in two large sips. To say my cock didn't appreciate the way her muscles worked all of that volume down her throat would absolutely be a bold faced lie.

I've never waxed poetic about the slope of someone's neck. Acacia, however, had me wanting to lean across the table and run my tongue along those corded tendons to see if I could make her shiver.

Fuck.

No. I did not.

There would be nothing past that damn kiss. It was why I brought babysitters with me. To make sure my very convincing dick shut the hell up and stayed safely tucked in my pants all night.

"You know damn well I always host a sunset tribute.

Hell, you knew how important it was because we spent the night together *two nights prior* where I told you how excited I was for the celebration and that I had a special guest attending. Yet, despite me obviously wasting any effort trying to engage with you on any level above primate, you clearly forgot about the entire thing after you got what you wanted."

The moment the words *spent the night together* were out of her mouth, my brain said *thanks, but no thanks* to normal, sensible thought. All I could think of was what would have happened if she and I really had spent the night together. That was a mistake. My mind took that as open season on playing out every scenario in my head that involved Acacia naked and splayed in my bed, panting and satiated.

"Are you even paying attention?" she asked, yanking me from the porn show in my mind. "How typical of you. You ask me for an explanation and when I give it to you, you tune out."

She crossed her arms beneath her chest. The shimmery purple dress she wore caught the lights and danced up the wall, giving off the sensation we were in a disco ball. I needed to think of something *stat*. Because I absolutely—though not intentionally—had not been paying attention and that did not bode well for the rest of the night.

"There's this little thing called the tide, Acacia. While an intellectual such as yourself might not understand the complexities of high and low tide, the moon determines *for me* when I can bring my boat to dock. If I miss that slim window of opportunity, my boat ends up on the rocks or stuck on a sandbar. You see, boats need a little thing called *water* in order to propel forward and backward. Without that tiny detail, we're just sandbar decorations for tourists."

I wanted her to get her hair up. To get her panties tied so tight that she'd start spitting nails again and remind me why she was simply a gorgeous wolf in sheep's clothing. Nothing good would come out of focusing on how sexy she looked with her hair swept off her face. Or how the purple-blue of her eyes caught the candle light *just so* and looked like the most rare of amethysts. The case study I'd been making of her face was the only reason I saw it. A drizzle of realization dropped across her features. First in the slight quirk of her eyebrow. Then, in the widening of her pupils and then the *O* from her lush mouth.

"I don't want this to sound insulting," I pursued. "But when I'm out on the water working, the only thing I'm thinking about is whether or not someone is going to go overboard and if they'll give a good tip. I know that Hemingway Day is akin to a high religious holiday...but to me it's just another day in July."

Acacia

WHILE I KNOW that I opened my dumb mouth and asked Edwin to have dinner with me, I was seriously evaluating my ability to make sound decisions. It had to be the drink. The reason that I felt all weird inside, like each cell in my body had its own heartbeat.

Certainly that weird feeling wasn't flutters. I wasn't surprised that Edwin made an effort for our date. No. Not date. Dinner. A truce dinner. That was all it was supposed to be. He wore a pair of khaki dress slacks and a dark navy dress shirt that highlighted the firm body my fingers clenched against the day prior.

Dashing.

It was the perfect description for how he looked. With his perfectly styled hair that managed to look windswept and not styled, and the scruffy jaw that he had to maintain to make it look so perfectly distinguished along his jaw.

"I swear, Acacia, I had zero intent to ruin your celebration. Why would I choose *that* year to enact my revenge? Especially after we'd had that perfect picnic just a couple of days prior. I wouldn't mess that up."

Recently when he spoke, my whole brain decided to forget all the reasons we didn't like Edwin. It was as if my brain repeated over and over again *Edwin the Supervillain, Who?* Instead choosing to notice stupid things like how he had a tooth that overlapped another along his bottom row of teeth. But despite that he had a dazzling smile that sometimes had me forgetting what we were talking about.

"Why do you call me *Sweet* Acacia?" I asked.

My tongue decided for itself, apparently, to hold a conversation opposite to the reason for my inviting him.

"The Acacia that is native to Florida is filled with pockets of nectar that not only attract birds but also rare species of butterflies. Including its namesake, the Acacia Blue."

He had to have googled that. No one knew about the Acacia tree or the Acacia butterfly. Not just randomly anyway. Unless, of course, you were raised by Dr. Demetrius Ashley, world renown etymologist and foremost expert on rare butterflies.

"My dad saw an Acacia blue the day I was born."

I smiled thinking about all the times my dad told me my origin story over the years.

"He said that if he was lucky enough to spot one of the rarest butterflies in the world on the day that I came into his life, it seemed only right that I get to share their name. Because I was a rare gift, just like a butterfly."

My parents married later in life and didn't think they'd even be lucky enough to have one child. Both academics, they'd resigned themselves to professional and academic pursuits. One day, I was their most thrilling surprise, so the story goes.

"Why a bar?" Edwin asked as he signaled down the waiter.

He didn't know what a flippant question it was. How the answer was far too complex for such an offhand question which he barely paid attention to. I went to Oxford just as my dad wished. I studied literature and pursued my own academic interests outside of the sciences as expected.

"Why a booze cruise?" I volleyed, not prepared to share.

He shrugged. I felt my blood pressure rise. That was exactly the reason that Edwin Wheeler and I could never have an adult conversation. Because rather than engage in actual adult questions and responses, he avoided topics like a teenager. His non-committal shrugs were enough to incite violence. Throw in the cocky smile and roaming eyes that accompanied it, and it could start another Cold War.

Those eyes knew too much. Saw too much. I felt flayed open. Like he could read every pump of my heart, or whoosh of blood through my veins. Each subtle sign telling him things he had no business knowing. Like how I'd obviously deflected the question, which he did in return.

"Look," he leaned back in his chair, crossing his leg over the other in a suave move I never would have expected from someone who scratched his balls as he piloted his ship. "I don't want to fight with you, Acacia. I never did. I thought that night when we got stuck on our inlet was the beginning of something. Then two days later you are burning holes into my face every time you see me."

"As I said before, you know exactly what you did."

"I ruined Hemingway Day. I know! But it wasn't

intentional. I'm *sorry* that some woman on my ship flashed Hemingway's granddaughter and then proceeded to retch, loudly, over the side of the ship as you were releasing your wreath into the water. You know as well as I do there was nothing I could do about that. Navigating the inlet, even if I can do it in my sleep, still requires actual boating. You saw what happened with the cigarette boat. Two seconds I lost focus and bam! I'm out a ship and an entire season's worth of wages."

That was what I thought I wanted. Why I brought him here. To reach a truce. To lay down our swords and broker some kind of peace treaty. That apology should have made me feel *something* then. Nothing felt different. Other than the strange vibration of every cell in my body making me jumpy and hyperaware.

Did Edwin always wear cologne? I couldn't remember if I'd ever smelled it. Fresh, clean—sort of like the sea, but if it were hugged with an angel's kiss that only bottled the good smells of the sea and left out the brine, the smell of fish and all the other unsavory things. That wasn't the only thing I suddenly inventoried in my head. His fingers? I don't ever remember them looking so elegantly long. Sure, they were calloused and a bit work roughened but I wanted to know what they felt like in places I shouldn't be thinking about while holiday elves ran around with bells on their toes and chipper people walked up and down the aisles singing carols. Someone at the karaoke stand started singing *Baby It's Cold Outside*. Just what I needed was a song about sex while I sat across a table trying to stay cool and unaffected.

"So, do you?" Edwin asked.

"Do I what?" I missed something.

"Forgive me. Truly. I'm sorry." He removed his napkin

from his lap and waved it back and forth. "This is my white flag of surrender."

"You said "Come to Papa!" and squirted more drinks from a water gun all over them. It was Candy Cane Key's version of *Girls Gone Wild*. Except with a bunch of middle-aged cougars and, well...you."

Edwin froze stock still, in the midst of selecting a breadstick from the basket. He stared at me for so long I almost asked if he was stroking out. I never in a million years thought I'd witness someone's eyes going molten, but they warmed to a gooey caramel color before nearly getting lost behind the jet-black orbs of his pupils.

"Oh my god."

His voice gave nothing away. Not surprise. Not confusion. Certainly, there wasn't a shred of excitement. But his lips quirked in that snarky, overconfident, swaggery kind of countenance that he sometimes had.

"Say it ain't so, Acacia."

"I don't understand."

The way he said those words? I felt them like hot syrup running down the length of my spine. I wanted to bend into the sensation, to writhe in my seat if it would extend the pleasurable sensation.

"You're *jealous*."

Pleasurable sensation officially quashed.

ACACIA ASHLEY JEALOUS? That was unexpected. And flustered that I called her out? An even more delicious development for the evening.

"Jealous? Please. Over what?"

She took a sip from her drink. It was a valiant attempt. Except I saw the way her hand shook. There was no way she was nearly as unaffected as she pretended to be. The way she licked her top lip four times? It was as if she forgot she'd already done that action and wanted to make sure just in case to moisten it again.

"Acacia, it's all a show. You know, so they have a good time. Hopefully they'll come back to me the next time they're in town. I give them what they want. And if a bunch of ladies are on a girl's trip where they want to be wild and crazy, who am I to stand in their way?"

Not that I cared two shits about my street cred or what people thought about me, but playing the role of the carefree, unattached, *mature* man I believed is what had people booking and rebooking. It was selling a fantasy. The cool guy who knew all the places to party, or the flirt who was never without a compliment or a fresh drink, the fishing expert or whatever it was my patrons needed to be. I was it. Whatever it took to make them happy and give me a good rating.

The waiter finally brought around a gin and tonic for me. From which I took two generous gulps and pushed through with an admission that surely had me dangling upside down by the short and curlies.

"When no one is looking, you drop cocktail shrimp on the floor for Six-Toed Joe."

The moment the sentence was out of my mouth, the pressing weight of indecision threatened to silence me. But I'd been silent for so long. That little tête-à-tête of ours drew on for too long over a misunderstanding.

"Call the Food Safety Commission—I gave my cat some table food." Acacia announced to the nonexistent audience of fellow diners that weren't paying us any attention.

"Every Wednesday, you wear your hair down." I press on, not giving any piece of fate a chance to stop the avalanche I started. "I haven't been able to figure out what the significance of Wednesday is. Whenever you wear those cute overalls, you always pair it with some esoteric *only funny to a few* literary t-shirts. But they're always covered up by the flap of the overalls, which also has always befuddled me. You buy the t-shirts because they tickle your intellect, but you make people work for a glimpse at them. Though I guess that is kind of how you are in real life, too."

I chanced a deeper look at her. Despite feeling as if my time is about to run out, I want Acacia to know how much I *know* her. Or how much I want to get to know her, if she'll let me.

"And you named a *bar* Temperance. As in abstinence from alcohol. So was it also a funny pun? Did you choose it because it's ironic?"

Statues shift more than Acacia had at that moment. It was as if someone poured concrete into her and she'd frozen mid thought. Usually, she was a spitfire of sassy eyebrow quirks or burning judgment in her eyes. And yet, there was nothing. A total blank slate.

Time punctuated its own passing with the jolting, grating lyrics of *Twelve Days of Christmas* from some gaggle of assholes that wanted to firmly believe it was, in fact, a countdown to Christmas and not the middle of July. Acacia and I hung in the silence of my admissions from *twelve lords a leapin'* all the way to *two turtle doves* before she finally snapped back to the present from wherever she'd retreated to.

"I don't understand."

That was the only thing she said. Her mouth opened and closed as if no air was able to pass through. If not for the heavy sighs punctuating the moment, I would have thought she was choking on her syrupy sweet drink.

"What don't you understand, Sweet Acacia?"

My fingers itched to reach across the table and play with one of those curly tendrils that kissed her collarbones. To gather her hand in mine and run my lips across her knuckles. Any kind of connection that would show my earnest hope that we could be more than adversaries.

It wasn't fear that held me back. Or even a chance at her rebuff. It was the way her eyelids creased, and her lips puckered. As if she'd drunk vinegar straight from the bottle.

Maybe I'd misread the situation wrong after all. Perhaps she truly found me distasteful, and I'd misread our situation entirely. An apology had begun to form on my lips when she clarified.

"You hate me," she blurted, her eyebrows raising in apparent surprise at her own statement.

"Never." I tried to hide my laugh behind a swig from my drink. "Do I have fun needling you? Absolutely. But I've never hated you."

She cocked her head in my direction, confusion still refusing to be evacuated from her features.

"And I hated you."

"Ouch." My unaffected chuckle feels fake even to my ears. She'd said as much all night long, yet in the abstract it didn't feel the same as her openly admitting to it. "Hate is a very strong word for someone who kissed me like she wished we weren't in public."

Watching her blush was my new addiction. That tongue of hers achieved Ninja status when it came to landing cuts and barbs. But the second I even hinted at the *suggestion* of something flirtatious, she was a blushing virgin.

Oh.

Shit.

No way.

Acacia Ashley could not possibly be a virgin. We were far too advanced in our years. If I had to take a guess, Acacia was more than likely in her mid-thirties. Was it possible? Of course. But surely someone as worldly and well-traveled as Acacia appeared to be had surely had a dalliance or two.

Jesus Christ. Being around her had turned me into a pretentious logophile right alongside her. Dalliance? Honestly. I needed a beer and a few hours of watching *Monster Truck Mayhem* to bring my IQ back down to *able to relate to others.*

"You kissed me, Mr. Wheeler. Please let's not engage in the rewriting of history after we've just laid down our weapons and announced parlay."

"If it makes you feel better to place the onus of that kiss on my lips alone, Ms. Ashley, then by all means, I kissed you. But there is not a smidgeon of a doubt that you enjoyed every moment of it. I'm pretty sure I still have the half-moon indentations from your nails on my chest to prove it."

Her fork sat suspended in the air, a piece of shrimp dangling from it. While she regarded me with her squinty eyes and quirk of her mouth, I watched that piece of shrimp dangle like it was deciding whether to fall back into the sea of rice on her plate or meet its fate between her pink, heart shaped lips.

Those heart shaped lips. The second my focus fell to the elegant shape of them, I was done for. Remembering how they felt pressed against mine made me desperate to feel them again. I couldn't see Klaus and Felicity anywhere. I'm sure they sat themselves in the "nice" area of the restaurant so they could bellow out obnoxious carols. But I toed dangerously close to tapping out and sending an SOS. Otherwise, I was bound to clear the plates between us in one fell swoop and yank Acacia's mouth against mine.

"You have a very inflated opinion of yourself," she finally said.

I shrugged. It drove her bat shit when I did. Silent gestures, especially the dismissive kind, were Acacia's kryptonite. If anything would have her going thermonuclear, it would be those.

"Whatever happened to Docker Danny?" I ask, knowing full well they went on less than a handful of dates three years ago.

"Come again?" she asked.

"Is that why you only went out a few times? Because you had to ask? Man. Let me tell you, for me, two is standard. I always try for three but sometimes the stars just don't align. I would have ended it, too, if you had to *ask* for him to satisfy you a second time. That's a shame. He had such an impressive collection of those shirts with the guy riding a pony. And they all paired so well with his extensive inventory of khaki pants."

Acacia went from flummoxed to flustered in a nanosecond. And that blush which had become so addicting morphed into a flush that peppered her skin from the tips of her ears all the way between her breasts. It would be a bold-faced lie if I said I didn't imagine what that flush looked like naked and sprawled across my bed.

"You are a pig."

I'd only ever seen Acacia really mad three times. Once when her liquor supplier tried to double the cost of her on taps without telling her prior to delivery and hook up. A second time when the Rochester kid—who came and did her social media for her once a week—wasn't looking when he pulled out of his parking space and nearly ran over Six-Toed Joe. And of course, when she came to read me the riot act after ruining her very somber Hemingway celebration.

That level of mad typically included a pointed finger, a jutted chin, and a frequent, angry, swipe against her forehead to keep her fluttery bangs from her forehead. None of those things were present when she spat the insult my way. But, I definitely unlocked a level above annoyed banter.

"Oh my god, Edwin ... are you on a *date?*" Felicity approached from behind me, her fingers wrapping around my shoulder. "When you said you were going out for dinner tonight, you never mentioned you were going on a date. MariJo is going to be so excited. She was just saying last night she wished you'd settle down with a nice girl."

My cousin and his fiancé clearly did not absorb the finer details of my plan. Namely that they were to wait for my signal and approach. Had I signaled them? Negative. I double checked my phone just in case in the haze of lusting after Acacia's mouth I sent an SOS. I had not. Yet, still they approached in the most obnoxious and saccharine way possible.

"I'm Felicity." She extended her hand toward Acacia, "I know you own the bar we were at yesterday, but I don't think we were ever properly introduced. You've met my fiancé, Klaus, though, I believe."

They sat down. As if they'd discovered the extra two chairs at the table Acacia and I had been seated at and thought *oh how serendipitous!* Felicity climbed behind my chair, yanked out the one directly next to me, and kept chatting as if she'd been part of the conversation all along. At least Klaus had the good sense to look apologetic.

"...used to work for a hot shot TV station....now I work for public access and make documentaries on the side. Has anyone ever done one on you? I think it would be fascinating. Girl boss owning a successful pub that is both tourist accessible and literary at the same time. You really have a thing for Hemingway, huh?"

Felicity and Acacia immersed themselves in a conversation faster than I could finish giving Klaus a dirty look.

Acacia

I'M positive I'd been beamed to an alternate universe. Edwin had tipped his cards and revealed far too much for me to be able to comprehend and digest all at once. And that was before his cousin and fiancé crashed our dinner. I felt adrift. Like the anchor that had kept me securely rooted in place had been severed, and I was cast out into unfamiliar seas.

Edwin *liked* me. Enough to be jealous over a guy that hadn't even registered as a blip on my radar of life experiences. He had a nickname for him and everything. Docker Danny. How he'd even known his name was beyond me. He'd been nice. Polite, inquisitive, doting even. But he found it distasteful that I owned a bar. Never mind that my bar was more elegant gastro pub than shack.

But Edwin had been harboring a judgement of someone totally insignificant for three years. Three. Years. Alongside that fact were the observations. No, they were more than observations. He'd made a case study of me. All the way down to noticing how I wore my hair. It was too much to take in.

"How did you two meet?" I asked Felicity trying to concurrently hold a polite conversation and suss out all these new Edwin developments.

"His brother overbooked their AirBnb last Christmas." Felicity laughed. "I walked in on Klaus taking a bath, then we got socked with a blizzard and well—"

She held her hands up in an *oh, well* gesture and laughed.

"There are a lot of details she left out." Klaus continued for her. "But bottom line being Christmas is now our favorite time of the year."

So much so that they were now on an island that celebrated it all year round.

"You're going to love the boat parade!" I told them. "It has always been my favorite. And getting to be this year's resident Santa, well—I'm jealous you get to experience that."

"You could have sat with me any of the times since Withersby stepped down," Edwin muttered into his drink.

"Perhaps if you would have shot drinks in *my* mouth from a water gun and suggested I *come to Papa* I would have scampered up onto that boat and shook my coconuts for all the oglers on shore. What a missed opportunity for free advertising of that booze cruise of yours. Damn. Next year maybe once you aren't competing with sexy Santa over here."

Felicity pushed out of her chair, shoving at Edwin's back to let her out. The move distracted him from shooting back whatever retort I could see trying to form on his lips.

"Alright, I need to hit the ladies' room, and Acacia, I think you would like to come with me."

She extended her hand toward me like we were best friends and would skip off in that direction hand and hand. I didn't take it. She didn't budge. She wiggled her fancy, manicured fingers in my direction, and I did my best impression of Sitting Bull.

"I don't bite," Felicity laughed, dramatically putting her hand out again.

"I would like to point out one small detail," Edwin interjected. "We *are* seated in the naughty section. For all you know, Acacia does."

Ass.

With a huff, I pushed to my feet and followed Felicity into the bathroom.

"God, the two of you. That is some tension with a capital *fuck me*."

As soon as the door swished shut behind us, she sauntered to the mirror to reapply her lipstick and check her hair.

"There is an ice cube's chance in hell he and I will ever hook up."

"If you say so." She chuckled around the lipstick tracing every bend and curve of her mouth.

"No, I mean it." I crossed my arms under my chest and stared at her reflection. "The man is a neanderthal. Do you know what he said to me?"

She raised her eyebrows as if to tell me to go on. I didn't need permission though. I'd totally warmed to my own plight. I was Joan of Arc carrying my banner of mortification over that hill to wave it in the sunlight like I was that little starving blonde girl from Les Mis asking everyone if they could hear the people sing while I waved my French flag. This is what Edwin Wheeler did to me. He made me mix my literary metaphors by a couple of centuries. Ugh!

"Earlier, I didn't hear what he said. And I asked him *come again*...and he told me *I would never make you ask*. And *I always shoot for three*. Who does that? Who says things like that? And honestly, I was asking him to repeat himself. I wouldn't ask about his sexual prowess in a *family restaurant*."

She threw her head back and her loud, throaty laughter bounced off the walls of the bathroom.

"Damn. That's smooth." She clapped her hands together, looking up at the ceiling and shaking her head. "I'm at a loss for words. Well played, Edwin Wheeler."

She said it like he was in the room. Or somehow would overhear our conversation and know she complimented his...whatever it was she was complimenting. Aghast. It was the only word that fit the situation.

"Klaus told me last night that he'd never seen Edwin act like he'd seen him at your bar. He tracked you like a deer in a winter forest. Every time we looked up, he was looking at you. I have no idea what happened between the two of you, but Jesus. The look he gave you made *me* clench, and I have Klaus giving it to me on the regular. I was squirming watching *him* watch *you*. And I mean that in the kind of squirm that ends with a night panting and sated after getting dicked so hard you came five times."

Alternate. Reality.

In what world did near strangers talk to you as if you'd been best friends since kindergarten? And who openly talked about their sex lives? But...*five times*. That had to be a load of shit. Five?

"How is that even possible?"

I didn't realize I'd said it out loud.

"Girl. I thought Klaus was a magician until I talked to my sister. *Her* husband Bryce? He has turned making her come into a sport. Like it's a point of pride for him how many times he can in one session. I think he had her at some ungodly number like eight or ten."

Rather than notice the fact that I was both utterly gobsmacked, while concurrently mortified, Felicity simply continued to plow through whatever walls of personal respectability I'd secured myself within and pushed right on through.

"Sorry. I know. I *know* you don't know me like at all. But how old are you? Thirty-five ish?"

I nodded. How she was so spot on was beyond my capacity of comprehension. But, maybe in whatever alternate reality I existed in at that very moment had also given people superpowers to determine everyone's age.

"I knew it. My sister and I are thirty-six. Klaus just turned forty-three, and Eddie will be right behind him in a few months. So, you know. Our thirties aren't meant for us to be ashamed of our bodies anymore. That was what our twenties were for. Klaus taught me that. Well, not the whole approach random women in the bathroom and talk about orgasms, but to not be ashamed of things that turn me on. Our bodies are built to have sex and to enjoy it. Period.

And if I can't sit here in a bathroom and tell you with absolute certainty that taking a ride on the Edwin Wheeler hobby horse will undoubtedly be as close to experiencing nirvana as you will ever be. Mark my words. Especially based on his cocky little promise, and the fact that clearly it runs in the family."

When I was a kid, I'd always wanted to be in the Girl

Scouts. My best friend at the time, Riley Cohburn, was a Girl Scout, and she would always come home with all of these awesome patches she earned for *being a good citizen* and *learning first aid*. At that moment, as I followed Felicity out of the bathroom, I felt like I needed a patch that said *I survived my first awkward bathroom conversation talking about my sex life with a stranger*. Yay, me.

"Hey...you hoo!" she called to some random person seated at the bar. "I know you."

The woman looked like she stepped out of a Disney movie. Long blonde ringlets for hair, gigantic blue eyes framed with a shock of elegant and full eyelashes. She sat next to a man covered in tattoos. The pair couldn't have been more opposite, yet they were so enthralled with one another, they missed the three times Felicity tried to introduce herself to them.

"The two of you look so familiar." She said again, touching the shoulder of the Disney princess. I half expected woodland creatures to come out of random corners of the bar and start singing about doing chores.

"Oh my god! I *do* know you!" Felicity's voice raised an octave easily. "You were at the birthday party for my sister. Well, technically it was supposed to be for both of us, but Bryce is a real bonehead and neglected to mention to everyone that Sera is a *twin* and therefore the *two* of us celebrate on Christmas Eve. Anyway—hi! What are you doing in Candy Cane Key?"

The pair—let's call them Disney and *Sons of Anarchy*—were yanked into hugs from an overzealous Felicity. I wondered offhand if she'd been served one of those figgy drinks, too. They packed a punch. I'd stopped at one because any more and I probably would have randomly been hugging strangers, too. Or worse, telling Edwin Wheeler how much I wanted more of those kisses.

"Acacia." She wiggled her fingers in my direction. "These are my sister's colleagues, Marley and Bear. Bear works for the radio station that my sister, Sera, works for."

We shook hands and exchanged awkward pleasantries.

"We're actually here looking for someone," Marley told her. "I guess he retired down here a few years ago. Maybe he's considered a local now."

Marley reached into her bag to pull out what looked like a worn *Playbill*.

"His name is Dr. Asher Krane. He used to work at Dartmouth. Now he has apparently retired here."

"Oh," I gasped. "I know Dr. Krane."

"She sure does," Felicity agreed. "He's a regular bar fly at her establishment. A lovely pub called Temperance. It's located down by the harbor, in the inlet. You can't miss it. He's helping my friend, Acacia, put together the Hemingway festivities."

I raised an eyebrow in Felicity's direction. She shrugged at me and smiled before throwing her arm over my shoulder. I guess I had a new friend. Apparently awkward bathroom conversations about one's sex life automatically bonds females together.

"It's going to be so nice to have another woman in the family. Don't get me wrong. I love Sera to death, but she's really the only other estrogen producing person we have. Sure, my brother potentially has a girlfriend that we don't really know anything about—but it would be so cool to have someone to look forward to visiting every time we come back to Candy Cane Key."

She steered me back in the direction of our table, before

seemingly realizing she never closed the loop with her friends.

"I'll see you guys at Acacia's place tomorrow. She can introduce to that Krane guy."

How on earth had the beginning and the end of the night diverged in such totally opposite paths?

KLAUS and I watched the ladies get up and scamper away to the bathroom. Felicity scampered, actually. Acacia looked as if she were being dragged to a guillotine and desperately wanted her own Sydney Carton to throw himself down in sacrifice for her happiness.

"So what did we interrupt?" Klaus asked as soon as they were out of earshot.

"Damned if I know." I downed the final remnants of my gin & tonic. "Maybe we called a truce. But it's possible we're right back to being enemies. God, that woman gives me a headache."

Klaus raised his eyebrow in my direction but said nothing. His accompanying chuckle didn't help either. Given I was an only child, Klaus and Leo were the closest things to brothers for me. And Klaus, being just a hair older than me, was the preferred cousin to his uptight brother. Which meant we'd been through some shit in our forty plus years. I don't think there was anything either of us had gone through or experienced that the other one didn't know about. Girlfriends, ex-wives in his case, life in general—we knew it all.

"Spit it out. I hate when you do that thing." I waved in his general direction. "I can tell you want to say something."

He held up his hands in mock defense, laughing the whole time.

"I come in peace," he continued, still chuckling. "I was just going to say it's probably not your head she's making ache. At least not the one that sits on your shoulders."

Wasn't that the truth. The second she cut me with her derisive, judgmental little squint she made me hard. The rest of the night I spent adjusting myself and hoping she hadn't noticed.

"And tell me what woman wants to know that her snappy little comebacks make me want to push her up against a wall and suck that venom right off her tongue? How is that an emotionally healthy partnership?"

He raised his eyebrows in the direction just past my shoulder. A signal the women were making their way back from the ladies room. He leaned back in his chair, folded his arms and pinned me with a look that told me he was about to say something I probably didn't want to hear.

"What self-help podcast are you listening to now? The reason the two of you are trading barbs back and forth is because you don't want to admit that you actually *like* her. For some reason or another in this stupid war between you, you decided it was better to fight with her than say you're fucking sorry like an adult and find out how to rectify it. And she's just as stubborn and pigheaded as you are, apparently. Since instead of actually negotiating a truce, you've been sitting here for the better part of two hours spitting insults back and forth. Pay the bill and thank her for coming to dinner."

He held up his hand before I could even point out that she invited me to dinner so she should thank me for coming. I'd still pay the bill—but that point should be noted. *She* wanted a truce dinner. It was *her idea* to meet here and talk about getting over this animosity.

"I don't care what the situation is that brought you into this establishment." Klaus continued. "Just thank her and let her know you appreciate the olive branch. Then go home and really think about what she said."

Shouldn't she be thinking about why she got so upset over something that was nearly unpreventable on my side? I ran a booze cruise. I had drunk people on my ship. The tide just happened to be pulling back just as her ceremony commenced. Of course, I never intended for her to be embarrassed in front of Hemingway's family, but that was out of my control. The drunk lady on my boat was nothing more than another customer in a long line of them.

I threw down enough money in cash to cover the bill and a very nice tip. Klaus and I met the ladies in the aisle. In heels, there were only a few inches that separated the two of us height wise. Though, despite the slight difference, she still cast her eyes up to look at me, surprise widening her eyes and making those sensuously full eyelashes of hers the perfect frame for her lovely blue lavender eyes.

"Thank you for the dinner invitation."

Despite feeling as if my insides had been sent through a woodchipper, the smile that I felt spread across my lips was genuine. It took three full breaths before Acacia smiled in return. Though I was being generous calling it a smile. For all I knew, the Greek food gave her gas.

"Acacia, it was so much fun having a drink with you. I'm really looking forward to getting to know you better."

Felicity yanked Acacia into a hug that, based on the pleading look that sprung across her face, was wholly unexpected and probably a bit unwelcomed.

"We're going to take a walk around town." Klaus pointed over his shoulder to the exit. "Acacia, it was nice to see you again. Thank you for letting us crash your dinner. Ed, I'll see you back at your place."

The pair shot out of the restaurant like they'd seen the ghost of Ed McMahon carrying an oversized check down the street with their name on it.

"Can I walk you to your car?" I asked Acacia.

Her distrust of my motives stung. She looked me up and down, a questioning look that had me wondering exactly what she thought I would do in the eleven steps it would take to reach her sensible little Honda.

"I'm just outside," she told me, pointing toward where her car sat directly beneath a streetlamp.

"Me, too." I extended my hand, silently praying she'd just take it without kicking up a fuss. "But rather than stand awkwardly in the reception area of the restaurant to say goodbye in front of a million eyeballs with loose jaws—I thought maybe I could say goodbye to you outside."

"It's fine." She pulled her hand back as if even being within a close proximity to mine would cause some kind of fungus to grow on her fingers. "There's no need. Thank you for coming to dinner. If you let me know how much I owe you, I can stop by tomorrow with my share."

For someone in heels, she sure made it out the door and into the parking lot quickly. Not that I looked anything like the guy, but I began to feel like Prince Charming chasing

after Cinderella with a damn glass shoe. Except my shoe
was the apology and olive branch comment Klaus suggested
I make. Clearly, the woman was dead set on getting any kind
of closure.

"Acacia..."

"Really. I see your truck parked all the way over there."
She pointed to the seven cars between her car and mine.
"You don't need to walk me to my car. I'm good. I'll see you
around."

She was so busy craning her neck that she didn't see
some idiot kid whipping around the corner of the parking
lot in his parent's golf cart.

"Acacia!" I yanked her arm, getting to her mere seconds
before that asshole clipped her from behind.

"Jesus. That punk almost took you out!"

I had a string of things I wanted to say after that. But the
soft press of her breasts against my chest, the feel of her
hands on my shoulders—a shower of sensation stole every
thought from my body. I was biology and nothing more. The
subtle scent of her delicately floral perfume teased me into
shifting even closer to her pulse point. That allowed me to
hear an almost non-existent gasp when my hardness lined
up with where she was soft and needy.

Her mouth was millimeters away from mine. Every
single nerve ending in my body implored me not to fuck up.
I didn't want to fuck up. But after spending two hours in the
spin cycle of sexual tension, I didn't know which path to
take in the forked metaphorical road. God, I wanted to taste
her mouth again. After all that bickering, would she still
taste sweet, feel soft and pliable in my arms, shiver if I
pressed against her harder?

The back of Acacia's dress draped low, exposing her

shoulders clear past the points of her shoulder blades. A scandalous cut for Little Miss Sensible. It was purely by accident that my fingertips grazed that exposed skin. But that tiny point of contact elicited a full bodied shiver that pressed the rounded notch of her cleft directly against the head of my throbbing cock. Her eyes widened, her mouth opened just enough to see the tantalizing peek of her tongue, and my control snapped.

Once again, I found myself pressing my hips against hers. Her ass pressed against the door of her car. In the breadth of space between our bodies colliding and our mouths battling, I heard a rumble break up the back of her throat that sounded husky and full of unspent need. That sound alone was like the red flag being waved in front of a bull.

I wanted to feel that rumble against my tongue. Savor the feel of her throat as she whispered my name and threw her head back. Her fingernails pressed into my shoulders as she keened my name and pushed into my body with ardor.

"Oh god, Edwin." She practically growled in my ear.

It couldn't have been more than a few minutes. But it felt like an eternity of bliss. The silken feel of her lips against mine. The warm welcome of her mouth embraced the sweep of my tongue. Feeling her open her legs inch by inch so as to get the head of my cock exactly where she needed it most.

Come back to my place. The words were on my tongue. Every time I tried to give voice to them, she'd dive in for another heady kiss, and the invitation would become unmoored, lost in the heated pool of desire we both waded in.

"Get a room!"

An SUV full of teenagers honked as they zipped past us,

screaming obscene suggestions as they did. I tried to hold her face, to cover her ears and deafen her against their catcalls and juvenile humor. But it was like trying to bail out a boat with a teaspoon. They were successful in doing exactly as I feared. Acacia pushed off my chest as if she'd been doused in ice water. I couldn't confidently say exactly what words formed on her lips, but I didn't want to hear them. Feared, actually, that there would be some snotty comment about how I took advantage of the situation or kissed her when she didn't want me to, and I felt too raw and exposed to be able to tolerate another barb after going eleven rounds with her.

"Thank you for the olive branch."

With her face cradled between my palms, I pressed one final lingering kiss to her mouth before wishing her goodnight and heading off in the direction of my car.

Acacia

IT TOOK me a solid fifteen minutes of sitting in my car panting before I finally came back down from whatever corner of the stratosphere making out with Edwin had shot me to. It was just a kiss. Fine. More like twenty heated, passion filled kisses that felt as if my soul had become disconnected from my body, and Edwin had sucked it out like a kid with a milkshake and a straw.

I wanted more. Every fiber of my being, down to the cellular level, strained with an insatiable need to find out exactly how Edwin Wheeler could mollify whatever witchcraft had overtaken my body with that kiss. Each blood cell seemed to have a mind of its own. None of them operated in tandem as if they floated through my veins playing chicken with one another.

I vibrated. My whole body tingled, and all I could think about was the feel of Edwin's hands on my back. The memory of his lips taking inventory of every bump, dip, and ridge of my lips felt like I'd dreamed it. And let's not even talk about the heat he was packing behind those well-pressed pants.

I wasn't a virgin. Not by any stretch of the imagination. But I'd never felt so out of control. My body and its reactions to another person felt alien and otherworldly. And that was before his cock started rubbing against my clit.

If he'd asked me to go back to his place, I don't believe I would have said no. In fact, I'm sure of it. So sure, in fact, that I found myself parked on Sandpiper Lane, staring at the light on in what I assumed was a bedroom in his half of the duplex.

His mom's half was dark with the exception of the porch light. I assumed that Klaus and Felicity hadn't yet arrived home. I'd cut the engine on my car ten minutes prior and told myself at least six times that it was now or never. I needed to sack up and march myself to the front door and tell Edwin exactly what I wanted from him. Yet I continued to remain cemented in my seat watching his shadows play against the curtains.

The longer I sat, the more time studious, proper little Acacia had the opportunity to infiltrate through the haze of desire. She reminded me in the same Catalonian accent as my mother, that proper ladies did not ring on men's doorbells with the intent of getting laid. Though my mom would never use the word *laid*. She would simply say something like "if a man is interested, Acacia, he will work hard to earn that claim. Don't give it to him for free. Then he'll be lazy and not think you're worth the effort."

Curiosity won out which shocked me. I was out the door and sauntering up his sidewalk before my brain caught on to my body's actions.

Call it curiosity, attraction, or perhaps total ineptitude

as to realizing when you're getting sandbagged and lined up to be another notch on Edwin Wheeler's bedpost. Regardless of the *what,* my body wanted to experience everything his kisses and caresses promised. As much as the thought made me uneasy, I also felt the heat of desire pulse through every capillary in my body.

Edwin yanked open the door, shirtless with a pair of pajama pants hanging low on his hips.

"Acacia?"

Seeing him in shorts and t-shirts every day had given me peeks into his lean form. Nothing, however, prepared me for getting an eyeful of the expanse of his defined chest and soft but not flabby belly. My fingers itched with the need to run my nails down his chest and feel the warm press of his skin.

"I'm sorry."

Words began to tumble out of my mouth. Totally nonsensical. I don't know what I planned to say when I walked up to his door, but seeing his chest, the lazy slouch of his cotton pajamas, his defined hip bones, and the soft thatch of hair that traveled from his belly button below the waistband to the cock that stood in relief against that thin cotton barrier—my brain short circuited. I had words. Lots of them. Spent years learning about how to string them together in the best ways to get your point across. But standing there on Edwin's porch, I forgot what my intention was.

"I should have probably just waited until tomorrow. But I wanted to see you. I messed up. Earlier. When you kissed me. Or probably I kissed you. Regardless, I should have asked you to come back to my house. Or who knows. Something better than standing there, stunned that you were kissing me. Maybe you're still interested. I don't know.

Nothing makes sense. Was it just the heat of the moment? And now, here I am looking at you in your pajamas who knows maybe you've suddenly realized that you don't actually want to sleep with me—" I practically growled with frustration.

Nothing that I wanted to say found its way from my brain to my mouth. Instead, I sounded akin to my seventeen-year-old self, the one who called every boy in my class to see if they were interested in going to prom with me. Only to be turned down each time.

My own existential crisis didn't phase Edwin. I barely had my monologue complete, and I was in his arms and he kicked the door closed. His mouth crashed against mine. The moment the two of us joined, my brain logged off for the night and turned the keys of my body over to sensation. Mouths and tongues weren't enough to dampen the fire that suddenly flashed in my veins and shot through my body.

"Jesus, Acacia." Edwin's fingers tangled in my hair, his lips traced along the bend of my jaw before making the journey up to my ear lobe. "Tell me I didn't pass out drunk in my bed. This is real? You're really here, in my house?"

We didn't come up for air long enough to answer. My dress ended up somewhere as I followed him up the stairs to his bedroom, not caring whether or not I survived the climb up the stairs with barely a glance at my feet or the stairs.

"No. Stop." Edwin pressed his palm flat against my collarbone just as I was about to follow him on to the oversized king bed. "I've waited so long for this."

His words sent a gentle caress all the way to my soul. It had to be a line. Something to mollify the book nerd so she didn't change my mind at the last minute.

"Show me how beautiful you are."

There were so many emotions tied to that statement. But every objection that knocked against my inner psyche flew right out the window. Edwin Wheeler, propped against his headboard, lust weighing down his eyelids and slackening his jaw, manhandled the outline of his cock through his pajama pants. Just seeing the *suggestion* of how turned on he was had my insides turning to jelly.

I was not the most feminine woman. Most of my clothes leaned toward function versus beauty. My bras and panties were mostly from Target, occasionally I'd grab a cute set from Victoria's Secret if I got drawn in by an ad fed to me on social media. But I never would be the kind of girl to drop hundreds on fancy lingerie with a French name. With one exception. A black lace set from La Perla gifted to me a long time ago by a boyfriend that didn't need to be named or even thought about. The gift, however, had its usefulness. Like while I stood at the foot of Edwin's bed in just a black lace balconette bra and a pair of cheeky lace panties that lifted and separated and made my ass look spectacular.

When I'd plucked them from my drawer prior to going out for dinner, I told myself I wore them for confidence. That if I wanted to form a truce with Edwin, I needed to feel powerful and assured. Now, watching him prowl toward me across his bed, I felt powerful in an entirely different way.

"Run your hands through your hair," he commanded, voice tinged with gravel that skittered across my skin and teased a riot of gooseflesh across my skin.

It felt awkward. Surely it was something I did every single day. I probably played with my hair absentmindedly nine million times a day. But doing so while imprisoned by the heat of Edwin Wheeler's gaze, watching him stroke his cock while I twisted the curls around my fingers and shook the bulk of my hair back behind my shoulders, it felt otherworldly. Seeing him, watching him watch me, suddenly the shy bookworm was doused in magic and realized all this time she was in fact the most beautiful, gossamer winged fairy.

"Just like that. Acacia, how are men not falling at your feet?"

His thumb traced gently from between my breasts, down the softness of my belly, to the banded waist of my panties.

"I have never witnessed a single man at my feet, let alone more than one."

I tried to smile and make it lighthearted. But saying the words out loud just reminded me of how little experience I had with men and being invited to their houses and into their bedrooms. And on the heels of that realization came the fear that Edwin would somehow find me lacking, and the shame that would result when he did.

"Would you like me at your feet, Sweet Acacia?"

Edwin slunk off the bed and knelt directly in front of me. His lips should not have felt as if they scalded every area on my body they touched. Yet, with every heated press, my own body surged to life in response.

"Is this the kind of apology you were waiting for?"

The rumble of his voice oozed sex. As if I stood beneath a waterfall and each of his words, the caress of his fingers against my skin, the soft kiss of his lips across my satin covered mound, were individual beads of pleasure threatening to drown me in a sensation I'd never stop craving.

Did I want an apology anymore? The word lost its

meaning. He had my panties rolled just at the top of my thighs, his lips centimeters from where I ached with need.

I wouldn't be able to stand through it. Especially not still in my heels from dinner. Edwin Wheeler did not just *perform* oral sex, he made love to my pussy with his mouth. The first gentle kiss and every muscle in my body forgot how to function. Each of them melting concurrently.

"Bed." He commanded, twisting me gently until we'd rotated enough the backs of my thighs connected with his mattress.

Edwin stood, gathering my hair in hands, pulling it away from my ear far enough that he could whisper in it.

"I'm not a fan of rushing."

With the grace of a ballroom dancer, he collected me in his arms, and swept me onto my back across his bed. His mouth worshipped at my ankles as he removed my heels, the clatter of them bouncing against his wood floors echoing through the room. His hair was mussed, pointing in various directions, a result of my fingers. Seeing that dichotomy play against the intense look in his eyes, had my body squirming in anticipation of what was to come.

That stupid drink probably had some strange concoction that messed with my body. I had never felt such an intense high simply from the feel of my underwear tracking down the skin of my thighs. Every sense was dialed up to a million. I swore I could hear the crickets singing outside, and the refrigerator kicking on downstairs. Edwin's heavenly beach smell wrapped around me like a scarf while I lay against his pillows. Even his comforter felt as if I prostrated on a bed of clouds and singing angels. Heaven. I existed in heaven and that was before Edwin's mouth made a topographical map of my calf, knee, and thigh.

"Patience, Acacia." He hummed, moving to the other leg and repeating the same process. "I'm sure there's a quote from some old famous literary windbag about how the best rewards come to those who wait."

His words buzzed in my brain like a hoard of fruit flies. I knew he was saying things, but I'd already careened past the point of caring about processing them. His fingers and lips had become both my heaven and my hell. The feel of them pure bliss but the need they created rivaled that of Dante slowly slogging through the nine levels of the Inferno.

While his lips drew patterns on my inner thigh, his fingers teased along either side of my cleft, tickling through my pubic hair, glancing softly down my slit before retreating to repeat the process once again. Edwin touched everywhere and caressed every place except the one that shouted and begged for relief.

"I see you shooting heated missiles from those launchers you call eyes." Edwin smiled at me across the expanse of my naked and shaking body. "You can give me all the dirty looks in the world, gorgeous, but I'm going to take my sweet time. If this is my last meal before my execution—I'll savor every crumb until sunup."

If he didn't start soon, his last meal would be a burned and blackened, combusted pile of ash.

Thirteen

KLAUS DESERVED a bottle of twenty-year-old bourbon and a box of the Cubans that Manny down the street sold to his favorite customers on the down-low. That motherfucker really did know what he was talking about. After leaving Acacia in the parking lot, I spent my entire drive home convinced I was the world's biggest asshole.

I'd wanted to text her. Or call. Something that said *hey I'm still interested, but I want to give you space*. But we weren't technically friends. Not like that. I only had her number because the island was so damn small I practically knew *everyone's* numbers by heart. But she hadn't given it to me. Or ever in the history of our friendship told me to call her, text her, send her a smoke signal. Nothing.

Imagine my surprise then when Acacia showed up at my doorstep looking sexy as hell with those wide eyes and kiss swollen lips. I should have asked her if she wanted something to drink. Or anything to show I actually cared about her as a person and not just a warm body. But the moment she delivered herself to my doorstep, the neanderthal in me wanted to lay claim.

Now that she sprawled on my bed, panting my name, something in me needed to make her feel so incredible that every other man that had ever had the pleasure to be with Acacia would be forgotten. Obliterated. To the point that Acacia would wonder if she was a virgin before me.

"Your skin is so soft, Sweet Acacia."

I couldn't stop running my lips against the silk of her thighs. And her smell? Heavenly. That didn't even cover the heady perfume of her desire that wept for me. My mouth watered knowing that was next on my list of places to explore. Those lips shone with her spent desire, and I was desperate to bury my face between her thighs and lick her clean.

With each pass of my fingers, whether it be caressing that pussy or tickling down her abdomen, she shifted and wiggled attempting to force my hand to her most erogenous zone. But the first thing to touch that needy clit of hers wouldn't be my fingers. And I had plenty of exploring I still needed to do before I allowed myself that delicacy.

I tried to ignore the vibration in my own legs as I pressed myself on top of her. My cock pressed against my pants, making me feel as if I were in compression tights and not loose pajamas. Acacia kissed me as if I fed her the very air she breathed. Her mouth crushed against mine. It was feral. Animalistic. Her legs opened wider accepting the full press of my groin. Her arms hooked around my neck as she gluttonously rubbed herself against me.

"Sweet Acacia has a naughty side." I chuckled, pressing my teeth to her neck as I cant my hips away from her ministrations. "Trying to steal what is mine to give."

Her frustrated growl only thickened my cock even more. I didn't think it was possible to become even more turned on, yet somehow Acacia did it without even trying. I knelt between her legs and pushed my pajamas off my hips, kicking them off somewhere in the direction of the end of the bed. Cock in hand, I savored the hungry look in Acacia's eyes, loving the way she struggled between holding my gaze and satisfying the curiosity that had her eyes struggling to flit down to take in length of me.

"It's okay to look," I assured her, taking a long pull from root to sensitive head. The sensation alone had me whiting out and desperate to fuck into the warm welcome of my own hand just to satisfying the desperate need to plunder.

"I haven't stopped staring at your luscious body all night. Turnabout is fair play."

I made a show of caressing my cock for her. Pinching my tip, pulling against my base, shifting my balls so she could take in the whole picture. She did more than take me in. She devoured me with a look that made me feel as if she wanted to make a meal out of me. Like that didn't puff up my chest.

Acacia had never been a person who faked anything. She gave it to you straight regardless of if you wanted to hear it. So to see her eyes go wide and glassy, and bite back a moan? I don't know if I would be able to handle this being a one and done if that was her intent. We hadn't even gotten to the sex part and already her sensual body and addicting brain had insinuated themselves into the marrow of my body.

"Do you like what you see, Ms. Ashley?"

Never had I cared if someone found me attractive. With previous lovers, I guess I'd always assumed they had, otherwise being in bed together would have been counterproductive. Yet, I couldn't help asking. I needed to know if she felt as out of her head as I did.

"I'd like it more if you stopped being such a tease." She traced a path with her toe up my leg nearly to my cock before I stayed her foot and spread her open so I could explore every inch of her pink.

It felt as if we were cradled in a room absent of sound, other than the surprised squeak that came from Acacia when I flopped between her legs and spread apart her thighs. It was my own fault. I spent too long teasing and winding her up that the game had the opposite effect, turning me into a rabid beast. The first taste of her slippery pussy unleashed a beast inside of me that had never surfaced with such avarice.

I couldn't let up if I tried. My mouth, my tongue, my nose, lips, chin, cheeks—there wasn't an inch of my face that did not get involved in taking Acacia to a height of passion that would have her nose diving into an orgasm so intense she'd squirt. That was the new goal. Whether she was capable or not, as I worshipped her pussy, I promised myself I'd die trying.

There was no better feeling than a woman's fingers in your hair, pulling and yanking, holding on for dear life while you fucked into them ruthlessly with your tongue. Acacia rode me like a prized show pony, cooing and moaning her approval.

"Oh, shit." Acacia's voice tremored and her muscles tensed. "Fuck. Edwin!"

Acacia coming was a glorious sight. Even in the low light of my bedroom, with just the nightstand lamp shining, I could see the deep rose flush across her chest inching toward her chin, the sheen of sweat coating her body, and her head locked against my headboard as her hips lifted off the bed.

"You went easy on me," I teased, pressing my fingers into her. "You should really make me work a little bit harder."

God, it was going to be glorious. Her walls clamped down and sucked at my fingers as I went in search of her g-spot. I reveled in the shocked mewls coming from Acacia as I found my target.

"Think you can give me another one?" I asked, already knowing the answer.

Her head rocked against my pillows back and forth. I could practically read her thoughts. She didn't believe she could, but I knew otherwise. Her tightly peaked nipples, her breathless sighs and moans, not to mention the nutcracker of a pussy that repeatedly clamped down on my hand each time I tickled that little bundle – she was going to go supersonic whether she thought she was capable or not.

Up her body I kissed. I took my time exploring her soft belly before making my way up to her glorious breasts. It only took a few suckles and nibbles before her pussy went from fluttering to contracting. I needed to taste her desire. To catch it on her tongue as she cried my name in ecstasy.

"Kiss me," It was a command, but one whispered in her ear.

I held my lips, just far enough away that it would take little effort for her to meet them. Her mouth was soft, the kiss far too tender given my hand was buried deep inside her, manipulating her g-spot. I expected teeth and tongue. But instead she kissed me as she would a long lost lover. It was slow and sweet, my face cradled between her hands, her nails tickling into my hair while she collapsed into the sensation of our mouths sliding against one another.

Just when I'd been about to whisper something dirty against her lips to counterbalance all of the sweet, she came again. Hearing her call my name like a mantra, feeling the rumble of her voice, and experiencing her come apart as our bodies lined up, skin to skin, her head cradled in the crook of my arm. It was too much. I couldn't protect myself. There was no more shield. She'd obliterated whatever protective instinct I had with her sweet *Oh, Edwin.*

No one else called me Edwin. I was Ed, or Eddie. The guys from college called me Wheeler. But Acacia was the only one who used my formal name who I never corrected or offered an alternative. And damn if it wasn't the sweetest sound on her lips. One I was certain I'd never get sick of hearing. In fact, I could say without a doubt I'd crave that sound until I was no longer able to hear. And even then, I'd reflect on what it sounded like.

I was so fucked.

Acacia

I DIDN'T KNOW which end was up. Or down. Hell, I couldn't accurately assess whether or not I even still had a body. What I did know is that the old Acacia no longer existed. Like a Phoenix she'd been charred to ash and forced to rise from that smoking pyre. How on earth was I supposed to go back to being a normal, boring human being after Edwin had just turned me into a sexual superwoman?

Not even bringing into consideration how well he could bring me to the height of bliss without even breaking a sweat, the man kissed like the main character in a blockbuster film. It was fire and passion one minute, and then sweet and coaxing the next. The entire world lay shattered around the bed, and the only thing I could think about was the delicious stretch of my body as it accepted his cock.

"I wish I could take you bare," he'd whispered as he pushed in. "To feel your skin to skin. Know the lush warmth of you inside and out."

The response on my tongue I had to bite back was akin to *fuck the consequences*.

"I think I'm about to combust," I told him instead.

"I'm right there with you." He rumbled right next to my ear, the flex of his hips stretching me in the most delicious, spine-tingling way. "Mmm, you liked that."

I felt his smile against my cheek, the wiry hairs of his chest tickling my nipples as he flexed his hips again, lighting up every nerve in my body with pleasure.

"I want to do this all night," he said. "But already I'm about to blow. You've reduced me to a teenager, Acacia. With your perfect smile, and luscious hair, the honeyed way you call my name. You're Arete and Aphrodite, my sweet butterfly."

He tickled at my intellect with as much surety as he coaxed my body. How he was still capable of words was beyond my understanding, however. The only thing I could say was *more*. I wanted to be filled and surrounded, to feed gluttonously on everything Edwin provided and then return to the table like Oliver and ask *please sir, give me some more*.

If I was nothing but a one-night stand, I wanted to make sure that I gorged myself. So that once I returned to my bed, and the only satisfaction I had was the battery-operated variety, I had plenty to use as material. Though I'm pretty sure after experiencing the all-consuming talents of Edwin Wheeler, I'd be hard pressed to find anyone even close to comparable.

"Edwin..." I gasped. Honest to God, I was certain my uterus clenched. "I think I'm about to..."

That was all I could say.

"That's what I've been waiting for," Edwin grunted,

pressing into me with hard, focused pumps. "You know that's what I want, sweetness. Take me with you."

I felt it deep in my core. A throbbing, fluttering, mass of energy that barreled down on me with little concern how it would obliterate me. My legs held on to Edwin for dear life, my ankles pressed into his very shapely ass, trying to brace for the onslaught. One moment I felt breathless, unable to even warn Edwin of what was coming. The next, a swirling vortex gathered me in its power, yanked me away from conscious thought and flung me so far and so high away from my body, all I could do was scream.

"So, you never actually did tell me why you named your bar Temperance."

Edwin and I sat on his bed– me leaning against his headboard, him sprawled across the foot of the bed. Our legs were entwined in the sheets, and we were eating ice cream. Of all the things I would have expected with an evening sleeping with Edwin, it wouldn't have been how soft his t-shirts were or how wonderful they smelled. How sweet he was post-sex. That he cleaned me up, got me a glass of water, found my panties, and gave me a shirt to wear to bed. Or even, that he assumed I would stay the night and not want to slink off back to my apartment.

We laid side by side in the dark for a while, just listening to the sounds of the water and the ambient noise of the island. Eventually admitting neither was tired. Which was when Edwin offered me ice cream. Since we never did have dessert on our date, he had winked as he jogged down his stairs and into his kitchen.

"And you never told me why you decided to open a business offering booze cruises," I replied back.

He sighed, pushing off the end of the bed to come around to the empty space next to me, which he crawled into after placing his bowl on his nightstand.

"Is everything with you a game of chicken?" he asked.

"More like a *I'll show you mine, if you show me yours.*"

He mimicked me in pose, stretching his legs out straight in front of him. The soft gray pajama pants were back in place, but it didn't slip my notice that once again, the cotton had begun to showcase the very piece of his anatomy that had blasted me into smithereens only an hour ago.

"My mom has always wanted to live in Candy Cane Key," He told me. "She and my dad always planned to retire down here, to buy one of the cute little houses that dot the shoreline over on Biscayne. They fell in love with this place when they came to the Keys for their honeymoon and decided that one day they'd live here. Then came me, and the general press of life—jobs, mortgage payments, sending a kid to college—and my parents always seemed to be satisfied living in Tampa so they were close enough to the Keys if they wanted to visit but still within a major metro city so that could still work. Fast forward to when it was time for my dad to retire, and he died about a month before he was going to finally say sayonara to good old Marine Steele.

It was bad enough that my mom lost my pop. I didn't want her to lose this dream also. I knew my way around boats. Figured I could easily sell my house and between dad's pension and the death benefits, along with the sale of their house in Tampa, I could set us up down here with a nice little life. Neither of us needed much. A place to live, and since we bought the duplex in cash, the only thing I pay is property taxes and whatever expenses the two of us have. My overhead for Three Sheets is minimal, so I can take care of my mom and still enjoy being on the water every day."

I think at that moment I fell a little bit in love with Edwin Wheeler.

"What did you do before you came down here?" I asked.

"I was a researcher for the Florida Maritime Historical Society."

Color me speechless.

"I had a teacher in grade school that used to say *to assume makes an ass of you and me.* I've never seen that saying so perfectly illustrated on someone's face before, Ms. Ashley."

His tone was playful, and the kiss he placed on my temple as he pulled me against his chest was full of warmth. However, it had to sting. My assumptions. The way I'd painted him as nothing more than a ball-scratching neanderthal.

"I'm sorry," I told him.

The words didn't even scratch the surface of the mortification I felt.

"What kind of research?"

He pulled the covers over our legs with his free arm while he continued to hold me against his side with the other.

"Sorry, Sweet Acacia. Witnessing me geek out on maritime folklore and the history of seaborn travels isn't first date material. You have to earn the right to get a peek inside my head."

My brain whizzed at a million miles a second trying to suss out where his passions laid. I needed to know. Wanted desperately to unpeel that layer of Edwin and discover what other things lay buried.

"I believe, in your own words, I showed you mine. Therefore, this better be quite the show, Ms. Ashley."

He leaned back, putting his hands behind his head, waggling his eyebrows at me.

"And if you want to share, while you're riding my cock— it's a hundred percent ready for round two."

EDWIN

I'D BEEN HARD EVER since I watched her lick ice cream from her spoon. Now every time she opened her mouth, used her tongue, or played with her lips, the only thing I could think about was cradling her head in my hands while she sucked me dry.

"My mom is from Spain," she told me, pulling her hair out from behind her and absentmindedly braiding it while she continued. "Pamplona, to be exact. When she was a young girl her mom, my grandmother, worked at the Gran Hotel La Perla, where Hemingway would stay when he was in town. She was fascinated by him. So much so, she studied hard, got good grades, went to Oxford to study the greats. Hemingway among them. She met my dad on a ghost tour around campus. She learned he was from Florida where the great Hemingway had retired to and the rest was history."

No wonder Acacia was such a rare beauty. She had the most intoxicating combination of genes. Her Catalan mom had a combination of French and Spanish genes, which would be how Acacia would have such arresting eyes and that luscious hair I wanted to rub up against like a kitten. She'd given me a peek into her life, and I wanted to bust down the door and make her a case study. To learn everything that had influenced Acacia in her life.

"That tells me about them. Not about you. And it definitely still doesn't answer my question about your bar."

I loved the delight in her laugh. Being the one who got her to throw her head back with genuine entertainment made me feel invincible. I wanted to ensure she laughed like that every single day.

"Patience, young Padawan. I'm getting there."

Fuck. And she could quote *Star Wars* right alongside all her big brained books? Every second she spent in my bed was another stroke of the tattoo gun ensuring I'd never be able to get her out from underneath my skin.

"My parents are both professors. Dad studies bugs, my mom prose. He is a research scientist, she teaches. Being the daughter of the *Doctors* Ashley set a high standard early on. Naturally, I went to Oxford and followed in their footsteps. Thanks to my mom, I loved Hemingway as much as she did. Maybe even more so. Eventually, I got a professorship at your alma mater."

Color me surprised.

"Have you ever taught college kids?" she asked me.

"Can't say I've had the pleasure."

She huffed and rolled her eyes, her arms crossed beneath her chest, the blanket that had been covering her breasts shifted downward, so it barely covered the tips of her areola. I refused to allow my cock to take ownership of my thoughts. I finally had a peek into the inner workings of Ms. Acacia Ashley, and a little nipple and her perfectly rounded breasts presented for my perusal would not sideline me. But

I would absolutely slide my tongue between them later. Round two was just on the horizon.

"Most of them don't want to be there. Maybe you get one or two that are willing to engage in some form of discourse but nowadays, most of the discussions about Hemingway surround his rampant alcoholism, whether or not he was a womanizer and a cad, and if his male privilege was the only reason for his success."

That still did not explain why she named her bar Temperance. I had to remind myself Acacia was never one for finding the shortest distance between any two points. Even if my cock throbbed with a host of tawdry thoughts of things I still wanted to do to her.

"Do you still teach?" I asked.

I couldn't imagine that she did. Her bar was seemingly her whole life. I wouldn't even know when she'd have time.

"Oh no. My teaching days are long behind me. After all that drama with Mason, I have zero desire to be within ten feet of an academic institution."

She said his name as if I had any idea who he was. Or what he was to her. I made a mental note to ask my mom in the morning. If anyone would know it was her.

"And when he caught wind I'd moved down here to open a *bar*, you would have thought I'd told him I decided to strip for a living. But he hated my study of Hemingway anyway. Hated that I had such a deep love for, in his words, a plebeian excuse for literary greatness. Coming from a man who worshipped D.H. Lawrence."

"Sweets, ya lost me."

"It doesn't matter." She tossed her hair over her shoulder as if it was the period at the end of the discussion. "The meaning of temperance is to find a middle road. To not diverge into extremes. To strike balance or find restraint.

"In my bar, I can choose to appreciate Hemingway, his career, the accessible way by which he told his stories, and their simplistic but poignant messages without being called plebeian, getting summoned before educational boards, or having to have my syllabi checked, cross checked, and triple checked before I could teach it.

"I can do as I wish because it's my bar. I answer to no one. Much to the great mortification of my parents who I am certain think I am experiencing a nearly ten-year midlife crisis; I love my life. And while my parents think I'm doing it to spite them, living here, charting my own course, I'm prouder of what I've accomplished here in Candy Cane Key than of any of the slips of paper that hang on my wall, or in any of my academic research.

"Perhaps I did name my bar Temperance because it's cheeky. But when I picked it, the true intent was more about striking a balance between passion and necessity, than intending to be ironic."

Her chin jutted in that defensively proud way she had about her. As if I was going to judge or criticize her for what she'd just told me. It was the furthest thing from my mind. She was amazing. I hated that anyone ever made her question herself and hated even more that perhaps our time as enemies had also made her feel judged or criticized.

"Our banter," I began. "I want you to know that I never truly meant anything unkind by what I said. If that is how it came across, I'm truly sorry, Acacia."

I gathered her soft mane of hair in my fist, and gently tugged so I could look directly into her eyes. If nothing more happened between us past this night, it was important to me that she at least know how sorry I felt if I'd only rubbed salt in already smarting wounds.

"You not only are impressively intelligent, but successful, compassionate. The whole town just thinks the world of you. I'm incredibly proud of you and the success you've had with your pub. Knowing what a big risk you took to strike out on your own, against the acceptance of your parents, makes it even more brave and inspiring.

"The truth is, bantering with you has been the highlight of my life these past five years. It allowed me to stay near you, even if you were hissing at me and throwing barbs in my direction."

The truth of that statement resonated to my core. Fucking Klaus. He loved to be right. And he'd landed a double bullseye with that observation. Thinking about Klaus had me realizing that it was beyond late, and I didn't remember them ever coming home.

Klaus: Based on the sounds from the front door we assumed you didn't want company. We're at MariJo's.

THAT WOULD BE an interesting explanation over breakfast in the morning.

"Is that your cousin?" Acacia asked.

Her cheeks were tinted a subtle pink. I'd made her blush. She didn't even have to acknowledge my apology. Just seeing that little hint of delight pleased the hell out of me.

Maybe we finally had set down our weapons and officially called a truce.

"It is," I said. "They didn't want to interrupt. They went next door to my mom's."

"Oh god." She buried her face between her hands. "Your mom is going to know that we had sex."

I leaned over and switched off the light, wrapped my arm around Acacia's waist and snuggled us both down beneath the covers. Feeling her warm body pressed against mine, the scent of her hair, and the slow relaxed cadence of her breathing was more successful at relaxing me than my favorite sleep app. Having her with me was definitely something I could easily get used to.

"She's deaf in one ear." I told her, smiling against her temple. "I promise you she didn't hear us."

Even if she had she'd probably be thrilled that I finally went on an actual date.

"You don't think she'll wonder why your cousins are sitting at her breakfast table in the morning?"

"Well then," I nipped at the tendon along her neck before rolling on top of her, pinning her with my hips. "We may as well make sure that all your needs are fully tended to. Mama would be mortified if she thought I wasn't a good host."

I didn't give her a second to argue. I dove beneath the covers intent on letting the whole neighborhood know who exactly was screaming my name in apogee.

Acacia

"NO. No! Not over there. We need you to put the podium over there, to the left of the bar, you imbeciles! That is the focal point of the entire evening. Why would we put it by the front door when the *water* is what we want everyone looking at."

Dr. Asher Krane stomped through the bar shouting orders at anyone who dared spend more than thirty seconds doing nothing. The guys from the playhouse had come down with their P.A. system like they did every year, and yet Asher suddenly took offense to everything they did. With the Hemingway tribute only a day away, he looked as if he would expire beneath the weight of his plans.

"What is with this wind?" Asher approached, tossing his clipboard onto the bar with a noisy clatter. "You may need to pull down your open-air windows. I can't risk all of these decorations getting strewn about."

He flicked his hand in the general direction of the tables behind him. I know it bothered him that I was nowhere near as apoplectic as him. I probably should have been. But cucumbers had begun to envy me, I was so chill. Of course, sex with Edwin, twice, would do that to a gal.

Just thinking about him and what we'd done the night before brought the heat back to my cheeks.

"Ms. Ashley, I know I told you to go and have fun with Mr. Wheeler—but could you please refrain from daydreaming right now. This is very important. The flower shop didn't have lilies and banana leaves for your wreath. They're wondering if palm fronds and freesia would be okay. But freesia is so small and delicate. It will break apart the moment it hits the ocean."

The tribute was my big day. My contribution to drawing the tourists in. Yet I couldn't find a single thread of concern over the seemingly important things going wrong around me.

"Ohmigod, he dicked you *real* good, didn't he?" Felicity skipped into the bar, beelining straight for me. I recognized her friends Disney and *Sons of Anarchy* approaching at a much less frenetic pace.

"Felicity!" I giggled, tossing my towel at her.

"Did he now?" Dr. Krane paused in the middle of chiding the servers about the way they presently rolled the napkins around silverware to insert himself into our conversation.

"We had to sleep at MariJo's house last night." She winked at Asher. "And it wasn't because Edwin's house was being fumigated."

The man with the tattoos whose name I remembered was *Bear* cleared his throat, obviously as uncomfortable as I was discussing my personal details with the group.

"Oh! Yeah." Felicity turned to them. "Acacia, you

remember my friends from last night, Marley and her husband Bear."

We all nodded our good afternoons, and the three of them took a seat on the stools in front of me.

"This place is beautiful." Marley turned in her stool to take in the full extent of my pub. "I love all the dark wood."

"It reminds me of this place in Spain we went to." Bear continued for her, "This bar that almost looks like it will be a hole in the wall on the outside, but then you go in and it's just unbelievably spacious."

"Yes, the Café Iruna," Dr. Krane recalled "Acacia's mother is from Pamplona, and I'm certain it had some influence. Though, having been to both, Temperance is unrivaled. Both in the food and the company."

I preened. While I never actively sought anyone's approval, hearing Dr. Krane's compliments warmed me. Sure, he spent a lot of time here, and I assumed it was because he enjoyed my bar—you never truly know for sure.

"Dr. Asher Krane?" Marley asked, sliding off her stool and inching closer to where he stood toward the end of the bar.

"I am. And you are?" he asked, extending his hand.

I saw it. Mere seconds before Marley introduced herself. It was in the way they both cocked their heads and considered one another.

"Did you work at Dartmouth?" She inquired "As the director of the Shakespeare festival?"

It was Asher's turn to preen. And if he'd been a peacock, his entire plume would be on display. A look of total pleasure that washed away the consternation wrinkling his forehead.

"Why, yes young lady, I am! How nice to have a fellow fan of the old Bard all the way down here."

Marley rifled through her backpack and pulled out the same tattered playbill she'd shown Felicity the night before. As she held the playbill in his direction, an entire story poured from her lips.

"My mom died a few years ago. When I cleaned out her things, I found a picture of her in a dress. I thought it was a wedding dress but it wasn't. It was from *A Midsummer's Night Dream* at Dartmouth. But my husband, Ted—this is Ted—" she wrapped her arm around his shoulders before continuing. "Ted found this playbill. The playbill where she tells *AK* that her cherry lips will kiss yours again."

I felt as if I sat in the front row at Wimbledon. All of us followed the conversation back and forth between the two of them. We all watched Marley as she spoke, and would pivot our heads to watch Asher's reaction, only to pivot back once again to watch Marley.

"She ended up dropping out of Dartmouth and moving to North Pole, New York, because she was pregnant. No one ever knew who the father was," Marley pressed. "But A.K. matched with Asher Krane, who was the director of *A Midsummer's Night Dream*. And I was born about seven months after that play."

The dots connected. Her suggestion hung in the air as if it were a physical mass that we all acknowledged. Asher had never been the stoic type. Not in the three years I'd known him. But witnessing Marley lay out the details of a sordid teacher/student affair starring one Dr. Asher Krane? I didn't even know how to react. I should have given them some privacy. At the very least offered my office for them to work it out. But I was frozen. Just as the rest of us were. Like a bunch of old *nonnas* watching our telenovelas.

"Asher?" I prodded, immediately regretting sticking my nose in.

"Her name was Joy," Marley continued. "Joy Jacobs. I'm her daughter, Marley. And I think you might be my dad."

I WATCHED Acacia and her crew buzz around the pub getting things ready for Hemingway Day. She glowed. Even from where I was perched by our shared grassy knoll, I could see her practically skipping back and forth as she laughed and joked with her team while they set up the pub for the next day's activities.

She'd donned a pair of well-worn jean shorts that showed off the legs I'd spent hours worshipping the night before, and another one of her esoteric t-shirts. Today's featured a pop-color image of Edgar Alan Poe mashed up with the *That's So Raven* logo. Fuck, she was cute. Seeing her in those next to nothing shorts had me wanting to sneak up behind her, bend her over her bar, and press my fingers into her from one of those tiny leg holes.

"D'ya hear? Storm's coming." AJ, our resident boat mechanic sauntered over from where he'd been tinkering on one of the boats in the harbor. He was sporting a red touristy t-shirt that said *Got my Holly Jollies at Candy Cane*

Key. Though there was boat grease all over his shirt, so it made it hard to make the full sentence out.

"Storms are always coming, AJ. I hardly pay attention."

I surveyed the collection of items I'd packed in the back of my truck. Everything for a perfect picnic. Big, fluffy blankets, an entire smorgasbord of foods packed in stay cool containers, fancy overpriced wine that needed special oversized glasses to allow the bouquet to breathe before enjoying. I received a full rundown of how to truly appreciate it by the resident wine connoisseur at the grocery store.

A glance at my watch told me I could steal away my new girlfriend in less than fifteen minutes for our date. Back to the place where it started. Well, not like we had to really travel anywhere since it was directly between our two businesses.

"This one's fixing to be a doozy," he said, rubbing at his sun kissed neck. "Say it might become a Cat One."

The weathermen in the Keys loved to shake their hands and cry wolf. It happened all throughout hurricane season. Every single storm cell had the potential to become a hurricane. And then everyone would panic, batten down the hatches, and the weathermen would be like *my bad* and shrug it off.

"When?" I asked. Though I couldn't care less. Summer in the Keys meant thunderstorms and rain. It was the tradeoff for a year of sunshine and blue skies.

"Late tomorrow the first bands might hit. Sometime around low tide."

As long as it didn't mess with my plans for the day.

"Boat parade still happening?" I asked.

"Far as I know."

"Then I'm not worried. The town loves that boat parade, and we draw so many people to the island because of it. I'd hate for it to get canceled because the weathermen want to be chicken littles."

As if sensing someone was watching her, Acacia looked up from where she'd been setting out binders and smiled at me. It had to be a first. Or at least the first time in a very long while that a genuine smile was directed at me.

AJ droned on about winds from the southwest. Those winds were apparently pushing the storm closer to us, but they still held out hope it would stay its current course. If it did it would skirt far enough east to miss the Keys completely.

He said more, but the moment I saw Acacia jogging toward me every other one of my senses shut down entirely. I couldn't think of another time I'd ever seen her look at me with excitement. It was a moment I intended to savor.

"Hey!" she called while she was still about ten paces away. "What are you doing here?"

Her head tilted to accept a kiss from me, without any regard to the prying eyes of the volunteers inside Temperance or AJ standing directly next to me.

"Thought I'd come and see if you needed any help to get things wrapped up before the big day."

Seeing the stress around her eyes dissolve and relief melt across her face made me want to pick up my phone and call every single resident of Candy Cane Key and tell them to kindly get their asses down to Temperance and help.

But I knew the whole town was busy getting the boat parade together for the evening's festivities and in the grand scale of importance, my little bookworm's Hemingway Day celebration ranked fairly low.

"What still needs to be done?" I asked, nodding my goodbye to AJ as I wrapped my arm around her and led her back toward the bar.

"Well, here's the thing. A woman, who is a friend of Felicity's, incidentally, came into the bar and kind of dropped a bombshell on Asher. Apparently, he had a love child he knew nothing about and this woman—her name is Marley—is his daughter. He kind of abandoned ship and is off with Marley and her husband. I'm trying to keep my head above water while attempting to figure out what his vision was based on his half assed chicken scratched notes."

Temperance was organized chaos. People flit in every direction carrying boxes, shifting tables and chairs around, setting out signs, and calling out orders to one another. It looked like a typical party set up: warming trays were being set out along the back wall with labels for each dish that would be served. I noticed all of the dishes' names. *The Old Manicotti and the Seafood. A Moveable Feast of Charred Summer Vegetables. For Whom The Buttered Rolls.* And a *Death* (by chocolate) *in the Afternoon* fondue fountain for dessert.

An entire meal of puns. Literary people. I didn't understand it. But if eating a menu that tickled one's intellect while also one's palate turned their crank, who was I to judge?

"I'm at your service," I announced into the melee. "Just start shouting orders at me, and we'll get it all done."

And that's what we did. Slowly but surely the boxes were unpacked, glasses were set, decorations hung, and all of the pre-prepared food was organized back in their storage freezers and fridges. The team knocked everything out despite the ever-increasing humidity and the resulting stuffy air from needing to close the storm windows.

Acacia stood at those floor to ceiling panes of glass surveying the choppy water.

"It's going to blow over," I assured Acacia, wrapping my arms around her shoulders from behind and pressing a kiss to her head. "And even if there's a little rain tomorrow, we can just call it Hemingway sending us a literary device from beyond. Everyone will eat that shit up. I'm sure he had some short story about rain and sorrow. We throw that into the mix, and it will look like we planned for it to rain."

Rather than acknowledge the plan, she simply squeezed my arms and relaxed back into my chest. The pair of us stood there reveling in the brief quiet.

"I'm so sorry, Edwin." She turned to look up at me. "It was wrong on so many levels to act like such a snob to you. You didn't deserve it."

"All of those demons were exorcised yesterday. Today is a new day, right? One where Acacia and Edwin are no longer enemies."

I wanted to say that we were lovers. The phrase was on the tip of my tongue, but I didn't want to lose the magic we had. I still had no idea if we were just friends with benefits, if the prior evening had truly been a one-night stand, or if it was the beginning of something. That was what the picnic was for. My date...our date. A fun and relaxed way to figure out exactly what we were.

"Think I could steal you away for a few hours?" I asked, surveying the last of the details that were getting wrapped up.

Acacia turned and looked at her transformed space as well. Seeing it through her eyes brought a newfound respect and admiration for her pub. She created that space against the advice of her parents and some guy named Mason that my mom had told me was *bad news*. Though she didn't give me anything more than that. Except when I asked if he'd hurt or hit her, she insisted that no, he hadn't. He'd ruined her academic reputation though, somehow. But she didn't have the finer details on that. Maybe Acacia would eventually trust me enough to give me the whole story.

"Has anyone seen Dr. Krane? It's been hours."

No one had. Felicity had to leave to go help Klaus get ready for the evening's festivities, but she'd similarly wondered before she'd gone where Marley and he had gone off to. Though I guess after getting a bombshell like *hey I'm your long-lost daughter from thirty something years ago* one may need to process that in private.

Acacia took my hand, and I led her to our knoll. The sun had yet to set, but once it did, the solar powered fairy lights I'd strung up would start to twinkle beneath the space I'd cleared for my blanket and picnic. I grabbed all my supplies from the back of my truck. The moment Acacia saw the blue checked quilt, glee and delight exploded from her as if she herself was a firework.

"A picnic?" she asked. "For me?"

Jesus. If she smiled like that for a tattered blanket and some grocery store wine and cheese, I'd give her picnics for the rest of her damn life. She gathered one corner of the blanket and helped me spread it out before folding herself into a seated position and helping unpack the basket.

With every item she pulled out, she oohed and aahed like it was the most exotic fare she'd ever been presented with instead of just little blocks of cheese and some crackers.

"A Latta wine?" She raised her eyebrows in my direction,

a sweet smile tipping the corner of her mouth. "Color me impressed. And it's even slightly chilled."

She gasped when I produced the special glasses the woman at the store suggested I bring. They were shaped like upside down bells. Apparently, they helped spread the wine out and capture the air that allowed the bouquet of the wine to blossom. I don't know. None of that shit made sense to me. But the woman spoke with such enthusiasm I just shrugged and told her I'd take two of those glasses also. Seeing Acacia's reaction and noting how impressed she was with my efforts made me want to sprint back to the grocery store and high five the woman at the wine counter.

"And the piece de resistance. What is a night enjoying Santa's boat parade without a little jeering of our favorite sexy Santa."

From my truck, I produced two gigantic poster boards. I'd purchased glow in the dark glitter pens to make sure that Klaus couldn't possibly miss us.

"Santa, I'm a naughty elf?" Acacia read, chagrin dripping from her voice. "Seriously, Edwin?"

I held up mine rather than provide her a response.

"*Santa, show me your candy cane?* Oh my god Edwin, you're the worst!"

There was no heat to her words. In fact she fought valiantly to keep a straight face as she chided me.

"Being turned into an objectified sex object comes with the territory of being selected as Santa." I shrugged. "If he can't handle the heat, maybe he shouldn't have agreed to be Sexy Santa."

Acacia

IF THE DAY had a chapter heading in the *Life of Acacia Ashley* story it would be *You Can Do Big Things*. Hemingway Day was going to be amazing. Something that truly would be a showpiece fitting his one hundred and twenty-fifth birthday. While Asher may have been the one to capture all of our ideas and put them in a semblance of organization that only he understood, all of the effort, exhaustion, and planning would be well worth it. Even if it was just a small group of us that paid homage to the literary great.

My team had really pulled together and leaned in. Something that wasn't unusual but always thrilled me to see how committed to one another and our pub they were. We'd done a rehearsal of the readings from various members of the town and a video slideshow of Hemingway quotes, alongside some more rare photos we found in the university archives. It was going to be beautiful. I wished that the Hemingway family could witness this year's event. But they'd declined politely as they had every year since *the incident*.

But that was behind us now. Edwin had apologized, more than once and in *very* creative ways that had my body thrilling at the remembrance. It was an unfortunate accident that we just needed to move past.

"I hope one day the Hemingways forgive me," I blurt out. Count on me and my dumb mouth to make sure to *Hindenburg* any date that bordered on lovely. And what a lovely date Edwin planned for the two of us. He'd recreated our first picnic, pulled me against his chest so I could recline against him while he reclined against a tree trunk, and fed me bite -sized pieces of cheese and sips of my wine.

"*You've done enough serving today,*" he told me, pushing aside my hair and worshipping my pulse point with his mouth. *"Let someone else serve you for a change."*

Edwin continued to suckle my neck, sending a bone knocking shiver straight down my spinal cord to flirt with my core.

"When you host your tribute, do you do it because you love Hemingway and want to share that love with others, or do you host your tribute so other people will notice you?"

I couldn't answer the question with his mouth on me. But it rattled in my head as the rest of my body surrendered to Edwin's commands. I did love Hemingway.

However, there was a part of me that wanted people to take notice of my event, I realized. I *wanted* that approval. As if having the Hemingways choose me would somehow prove to all those stuff shirts at the university that they'd thrown their favor behind the wrong professor. That Mason had been wrong, and my censure was unjust and unfounded.

"Maybe a little bit of both," I admitted, feeling a prick of shame wash over me.

"Hey, it's nothing to feel bad about. We all want to be recognized for a job well done. But what does having the Hemingways here do for you? Is it because you want more publicity for Temperance? Because from where I sit, your pub is quite successful. Maybe from where you sit you think it should be doing better because we all set impossible standards for ourselves in regard to our personal measures of success. My useless opinion? I'm in awe of you and your pub."

Feeling the weight of his arms wrapped around me anchored against his firm chest was quickly becoming my favorite place to be. I don't think I'd ever get tired of his ocean smell or stop relishing in the feel of his scruff along my cheek.

Boats floated by us, each one decorated in a holiday theme. Cheery songs blast from their stereo systems as they waved enthusiastically as they passed by. Being here in our inlet truly was the best, most private place to watch the parade. We got to see everyone first, as they turned toward town and the wild rash of people.

"When I was at U.F., Mason—my ex—hated that he wasn't truly considered part of the American Literature fellows. D.H. Lawrence was a British writer, you see. And though Mason argued extensively that his best works were written while he lived in New Mexico, he often found he was grouped with the British scholars instead of the American ones.

"It sounds stupid, I know. Now that I've been divorced from academia for so long, all of the bullshit just sounds so childish and exhausting. But when you're in an institution that exists on placing value on your contribution to academic conversation—where in that conversation you exist means a lot.

"And D.H. Lawrence was just as skeezy as Hemingway. Probably more so. Though I'm not an expert, and I'm not going to bore you with a thousand details."

"I can say this without any bullshit, Acacia. You are solidly the least boring person I have ever met." Edwin pressed his face directly against mine. Though we were talking in a totally normal volume, the privacy of our space made it feel as if we were whispering solutions to the world's problems to one another.

Edwin pressed a wineglass in my hand, filled once again by the delicious selection he'd brought. The whole evening had a warmth radiating through me that had nothing to do with my second, overly full glass of expensive wine, and everything to do with the sweet and caring man who existed beneath all that gruff sarcasm.

"Long story short, I published an article in a well-known journal discussing some of Hemingway's finer points. I didn't intentionally ignore his problems with alcohol and his love of bedding women, but Jesus, those points have been argued to death. It was well-received, and Mason didn't like that. Hated I was being sent to speak at an international literary conference about someone who he deemed beneath the esteem of literary discourse. So he published a counter piece. One that accused me intentionally of glossing over a problematic writer, ignoring current discussions about him, and deliberately turning my back on the very university that employed me. His hit piece also got some attention. Enough attention that I was called before the Provost. They questioned my syllabi, my essay topics. Every single item I taught in class was scrutinized and modified. They told me to take a sabbatical while they evaluated my place in the department and where my scholarship should focus the next academic year. During that time, Mason somehow wormed himself into the American Lit department and convinced the Dean to demote to me teaching Freshman English with monitored classes so they could insure I toed their lines. So I told them to fuck off and opened my bar.

"The problem was that Mason was in tight with my parents. And the three of them all during this censure constantly questioned my judgment and fed me their opinions on how I should handle the drama at the university. My parents sided with Mason! With Mason! Over their own daughter. My mother, especially, said I was too naïve to think I didn't have to play politics at any university, and I should be grateful I landed a job with such an exceptional institution. She insisted I needed to go back hat in hand and take my lashings."

It felt good to get it all out. I didn't expect that. But sitting in the quiet with the twinkle lights and the ambient sounds of nature, the excited laughter and shouts from the boats, Six-Toed Joe curled at the corner of the blanket staring at us—I felt free.

"You made the right decision." Edwin's fingers played in my hair, soothing my frayed nerves with every stroke. "And if it makes you feel better, I'll refrain from sending my fifty-dollar check to this year's alumni fund as a sign of solidarity."

"Wow. Your *whole fifty dollars*?" I asked, giggling as he pressed a kiss to my neck. "The university might collapse."

He shifted enough that I could see his face. His finger pressed against my chin, raising my gaze to meet his. The firm set of his lips and the forlorn expression weighing down the lines in his forehead had me worried for a second, I'd insulted him.

"That's what they get for crossing Acacia Ashley." he said, holding that stern expression for at least three breaths before breaking out into a smile and winking at me.

Our jovial bubble broke when a boat honked its horn long and low, catcalling to get Edwin's attention. It was decorated like a pirate ship, and across the bow was a banner that read 'Bring Back the Pirate Wheeler or face the cannons!"

"The Pirate Wheeler?" I asked, turning to him for explanation.

In all the years I knew Edwin, I don't think I'd ever seen him blush. And it wasn't a flush that could be blamed on the wine, or the warm humidity of the night, or even the occasional gust of wind. His cheeks, his neck– hell, even the tips of his ears– had gone strawberry red.

"They're friends." He pointed toward the boat, looking nervous of all things. "They're being cute, trying to get me re-installed as Santa."

"Okay, sure. I can see friends doing that. But why are they calling you Pirate Wheeler?"

Instead of answering me, he poured the final remnants of the bottle of wine in each of our glasses before downing his in two inelegant gulps.

"Did you happen to see who sponsored that boat?" he asked, opening up the town's app and showing me the lineup of boats.

"The historical society!" I gasped, remembering him telling me about his previous work.

"I specialize in maritime history, as you'll recall."

"I don't understand how that pertains to..." And then it hit with what felt like a thunderous crash in my brain. "Oh my god. You study pirates!"

"Not just pirates, my little book nerd. I study the history of pirates and how they contributed to the formation of our democracy."

Edwin launched into a dissertation's worth of information on how pirate routes helped improve trade, which led to westward expansion, and how pirates influenced many pieces of American history. It was hot to be honest. He had a big fucking brain and holy crap, listening to him wax poetic about people I never actually knew existed in real life, had my brain churning on a totally different level.

"And there are so many books I could recommend if it's truly something you're interested in," he continued. "Don't even get me started on modern day feminism and how overlooked female pirate captains are. They laid groundwork for feminist thought and subversion more than many of the women credited with such today."

His excitement over pirates got stymied as the man of the hour appeared around the bend of the inlet. Edwin passed me my sign, forcing my hands far above my head so that Klaus would be able to read it as he floated by. Edwin did the same with his cat calling to his cousin and telling him how sexy he looked in his candy cane bike shorts.

Felicity was the first to notice us, cackling as she pointed at us and nudging Klaus' bicep to get his attention. The two of us, caught up in Felicity's delight, stood, jumped up and down, and made a total scene with our hero worship.

"Oh Klaus, you're so sexy!" Edwin called to him with a

high-pitched attempt at a female voice. "Come over to my place later, and you can come down my chimney."

"Edwin!" Felicity cackled, quarterbacking a whole bag of individually wrapped candy canes in our general direction. "This is a family show, you pervert!"

Though the words were barely discernible through her tear-filled laughter.

"Oh god, not you, too!" Klaus pointed toward my sign. "I'm pretty sure that was made very clear last night at dinner."

He shook his finger at me, shaking his head as the boat steered away from us and further toward town.

Nineteen

THOUGH CHILLY WAS a bit generous for the temperature, I'd lit a little campfire for the two of us so we could continue to enjoy the night while we waited for the fireworks to begin. It actually felt like a real date.

Opening up to Acacia didn't even feel scary. Telling her about my life, witnessing her listen to my passions and actually be excited to learn about them without shutting me down or having her eyes glass over, couldn't have been the more perfect scenario if I'd scripted the evening.

And she made me hard without even trying.

At the moment, her nose was buried on some academic site while she read about Ann Bonny and Mary Read. Every so often she'd quote some tidbit she found exciting and she'd look up at me and ask 'did you know that Mary Read challenged a man to a duel to defend her boyfriend?' I did know that. But I didn't want to dampen her excitement.

"Maybe once all the Christmas in July festivities are behind us, I can take you to the Maritime Historical Society. There is a whole installation I helped create and it covers a host of female pirates. I could bore you for hours waxing on about them."

She beamed at me. It was like the full force of the sun behind her smile. And it took everything in me to not pack up our picnic and drive the two hours to the museum and let her in with the door code I was certain was still the same from when I worked there.

"All this time I had a fellow nerd as a neighbor, and I never knew it."

"When you spend all your energies focusing on the things that you hate about a person—you tend to miss out on the little things that you might find are pretty cool," I told her.

I hadn't meant to make her sad or hurt her feelings. But the second I spoke the words she looked stung. An apology was forming on my lips when she tossed her phone aside and climbed right into my lap, wrapping her arms around my neck.

"I'm sorry, Edwin." She pressed a kiss to my mouth that despite the sweetness of it, made me ache for her to move on top of me just as she was with my cock buried inside of her. "I shouldn't have acted like such a snob. I did to you the exact thing I escaped. Judgement. Castigation. Forcing others down in order to feel intellectually superior. It was a shitty thing to do to a friend. And I'm really sorry."

I didn't want to rehash the conversation again. When I'd told her it was water under the proverbial bridge, I'd meant it. Now that I understood what happened between her and her ex, I understood with a little more clarity why an honest mistake could feel like professional ruin and bring back the same feelings.

It also meant that she'd liked me even then. Because if

her experience with Mason pointed to anything, it was that she'd been embarrassed and exposed by a lover. While she and I hadn't slept together five years ago, we danced around one another, being too cautious to just plainly say what obviously we'd both felt.

No more of that shit. Now was the time for *carpe diem*. Her ass fit so nicely in the palms of my hands and shifting her just the slightest bit higher took next to no effort at all.

With her lips against mine, what had been a sweet kiss morphed into something hotter. It was a slow building pyre on which we'd submit all our past indiscretions. Once it burned away the hurt, we'd come out the other end a pair of Phoenix ready to burn for one another instead.

"Edwin," she gasped, pressing her core firmly against my questing fingers.

"These shorts have been teasing me all day," I told her, tickling up her thigh beneath the leg. "I have been fighting the need to press you face down on your bar and worship this pussy while you bite down on my hand to keep from screaming."

Whether she acknowledged it or not, she liked the sound of that. I felt her tense. Her legs spread even further open, the warmth of her core tantalizing my groin. My fingers hadn't even met their target yet, and she squirmed like a virgin.

"Cock or fingers, sweetheart?" I asked, internally high fiving myself for tucking a rubber in my pocket before I'd left. "Or I can give you both if you think you can get off before the fireworks finish."

The pinch of her teeth scoring down my neck rushed blood from my entire body directly to my already throbbing cock. I made quick work of covering us with the end of the blanket, and pushing her shorts down to her thighs.

"What if someone sees us," she moaned, fucking my fingers as she did.

"You're covered by a blanket, and there is no one around. The fireworks haven't even started. We have about twenty minutes, beautiful. Think you can come for me? I've been dreaming about seeing you come apart again all day. It's my new favorite thing to watch."

I didn't wait for an answer. With two of my fingers buried inside of her, my thumb worked her clit in an attempt to throw her over into at least one orgasm just in case some unsuspecting fool stumbled across us. Her mouth fused with mine as she moaned her orgasm into my mouth, jerking violently in my lap as I drew out every last spasm.

"Would you like my cock?" I asked. "Or are you tapping out?"

Beneath the blanket, my fingers drew patterns up and down her spine, while her hips moved in seductive circles across my straining cock.

"Not tapping out."

She purred into my ear, her fingers cupping me through my shorts before finding the button and zipper. We worked in tandem to get me freed and sheathed with the speed and efficiency of a NASCAR pit crew before I pressed into her and covered us back up with the blanket.

"Why does this feel so fucking good?"

Hearing the word *fuck* coming from the mouth of proper, erudite Acacia Ashley was an aphrodisiac on a normal day. Hearing her say the word in relation to how good my cock felt buried inside her? I had to sing the alphabet in my head to keep from blowing prematurely.

"You feel so good, sweetness. If I could, I'd be right here all damn day."

She leaned back against my hands, allowing me to set the pace. I shifted her hips back and forth while she sighed my name and wrapped her arms around my neck. Her distended nipples poked through her brainy little t-shirt, making Poe look like he had two peaks for eyeballs. I suckled at her nipples through that cotton shirt, holding her at her upper back, and pressing her deeper into my mouth.

"I'm not going to last much longer if you keep doing that." she hummed, pushing herself even further into my mouth. "I never thought I could come just from someone sucking me, yet I'm about to fall over."

I worked her nipple between my teeth and moved my hands to her hips, holding her in place while I pressed up into her.

"If you think it's just your nipples getting you off, I'm a little nervous for my poor cock. You're going to hurt his feelings."

Acacia pulled at my chin so my ear lined up with her mouth.

"Aww, poor Pirate Wheeler," she teased, thickening my cock. "I'll never overlook the feeling of a good plunder."

Fuck. That dirty little minx. I promised myself one of these days I'd show her what it was to be properly plundered by a pirate. Unfortunately, she pushed a hidden button that I don't think I'd ever exposed to anyone, and I lost the battle of wills.

Acacia was on her back faster than either of us could process the change in position. I rutted into her like a randy high schooler getting his first handy.

"You better give me that come right now, Acacia."

I held her down right above her mound, pushing my cock up against her inner wall, and tickling her clit with my thumb. No way would I go over without making sure she was jumping, too.

"Come on, Sweets," I cajoled, trying to grit through the overwhelming need to blow. "Be my good girl."

That was all it took. Acacia flew apart. She arched off the blanket and shouted into the heavens. If not for the fireworks display covering the sounds of her completion, more than likely someone in town would have heard us.

It felt like hours before the two of us came back down. Neither of us moved or were even capable of doing so. Cradled beneath the blanket, panting and covered in sweat, we stared up at the ribbons of color that rained down on us with glorious, popping explosions.

"Edwin," her fingers tickled through my hair, before scoring down my five o'clock shadow. "I think I—"

"Acacia Ashley!"

Mrs. Soames and Wanelda stood near Acacia's bar. They were far enough away that they couldn't see anything besides us laying on a blanket, but their arrival shot panic through both of us.

"Who is out there with you?" Mrs. Soames called.

"I'll be right there!" Acacia called back, groping wildly beneath the blanket I assumed in search of her panties and shorts.

My shirt was long enough to cover my haphazardly buttoned shorts. I shot off the blanket to intercept them while Acacia tried to put herself back together.

"Mrs. Soames, Wanelda! What brings the pair of you to this side of the island. Don't the two of you usually sit in the Grand Marshal's booth?"

"Well, yes," Wanelda replied, "but Acacia never showed up and we got worried. We came to see if maybe she was still trying to set up tomorrow's festivities. It's all over town what happened with Dr. Asher Krane and that girl claiming to be his daughter."

I stepped even closer toward Temperance, drawing them further away from our picnic blanket and positioned the pair with their backs to Acacia. I watched her stand and shimmy into her shorts, trying not to drop my conversation as I watched her panties skim past her pubic mound and snap back into place.

"I came by a little bit ago and helped with all the final details," I told them. "We finished in just enough time for the beginning of the boat parade, so we decided to just watch it from here rather than try to make it into town with enough time to enjoy the festivities."

"Thank you so much for checking on me." Acacia leaned in to give them each a hug. "We're actually all set for tomorrow. All we need is the weather to cooperate, so if you want to stop by the church on your way home and send up an extra prayer, I'd appreciate it."

She gathered the two ladies up with grace and escorted them back to their little golf cart and waved them on their way. I'd been about to compliment her on her suave handling of the situation when I saw the storm brewing on her face. In three focused strides she was directly in front of me, her fighting face locked in place.

That damn chin always gave her away. I stared into the eyes of old Acacia, fire brewing behind those eyes. Her lips twitched as if a tempest was beginning to form.

"You always take things too far!" she lamented. She stormed past me to collect her things from the blanket. "We were having a wonderful time. Even the kissing could have been explained away. But now the entire town is going to be gossiping about how I spread my legs for you."

I tried to cradle her against my chest. To calm the fight out of her with a hug, but she wasn't having it. She jerked her shoulder against my chest and broke free from my hold.

"Acacia, no one saw you. I swear. I kept an eye out the entire time to ensure no one walked up on us and caught us by surprise. You were safe. You *are* safe. With me. I'll always protect you."

Rather than acknowledge anything I said, she called to her cat, making kissing noises and meows to get him to come to her.

"You never want to go at anyone else's pace." She continued once she'd gathered Joe up in her arms. "It's full throttle or nothing. And now because of it, I'm going to be a laughingstock."

"You aren't going to be a laughingstock. Promise. And if by some miracle one of them actually saw anything, I will do everything in my power to squash any rumor before it has a chance to start."

Our inlet was practically abandoned. Very few residents ever came down this way unless their boat was docked around the bend. Acacia, Me, Manny, sometimes AJ—we were the most frequent visitors of the space on an off night when we had no patrons. The entire town practically was down near the pier in town watching the parade. There was less than a half a percentage chance that those two old biddies could see or hear *anything* let alone the afterglow of our lovemaking beneath the loud boom of fireworks and in the dark.

"They're going to know that we were making out,

Edwin. Tomorrow morning the whole town is going to know about us."

Acacia's upset was clouding her common sense. In the morning, I knew she'd see things differently. But her panic clouded any sensible thought. And instead of telling her all of the things that I'd realize in introspection, I blurted the one thing I knew I needed to hold back.

"So!" I bit back. "Let them know! Hell, I'll shout it from the rooftops myself. Acacia, I love you. I don't care if those two old ladies found us fucking on that picnic table over there right out in the open. Let them talk. Have them tell the whole world. I finally, *finally* got Acacia Ashley to date me. You're *it* for me, Acacia."

The words tumbled out of my mouth before I could pull them back. Though true, I knew Acacia would not appreciate being firehosed in my truth.

"That is exactly what I mean!" She thrust her finger into my chest. "We literally just had our first date and you're already professing your love. How is that normal?"

The boats would start coming back to their docks soon. Even with as heated as Acacia was, this would only escalate to really bad if the entire town really *did* know that we were fighting about having sex in public.

"Acacia, I've known you for almost *ten years*. I've been in love with you since that day five years ago when we sat on this very spot and had the most perfect date. I'd say that this has been quite possibly a snail's pace toward this point."

I tried to take her hand, and she pulled it away. When I tried to get closer to her, she stepped back. We returned to square one, apparently.

"Look, the boats are going to start filing back in here any minute. How about I take you home, and we can call it a night. Once the embarrassment wears off and the morning brings a fresh perspective, you'll see that this will be something to laugh about."

She smashed her face into Six Toed Joe's neck, snuggling into his fur. After a moment, she took a deep breath, gathered herself up to her full height, jut that chin out and squared her shoulders before telling me, "I have my own ride home."

Somehow that one cold and aloof statement felt like the calm before the proverbial storm.

Acacia

THE FIRST THING I did when I woke up was check my phone. Surely if I was the source of town gossip someone would have broken the news to me via text. I certainly wasn't an early riser, but I assumed by nine in the morning all the old ladies having their coffee and danish over at the Candy Cane Country Club would have their chins wagging by sunrise. Not a single text message, other than one from Edwin asking if I made it home okay.

Screw him.

The moment I saw his name on my screen, I drifted out to sea on a torrent of memories. The night had been absolutely perfect. The best date I'd ever had in all my thirty-five years on this earth. Even the sex. Jesus, the sex. Otherworldly.

I shouldn't have freaked out on him. I knew it. But also, he *loved* me?

What kind of shit was that? He'd spent the last five years making my life hell, and then suddenly, on a dime, he is professing his undying devotion to me? I pushed off my covers and stomped into my shower, totally distracted by my careening thoughts.

Felicity: Hey! I hope you don't mind I got your number from Ed. Yesterday was so much fun! And I'm still cracking up over those posters. Jesus the two of you. 💀

Felicity: What time would you like Klaus and I to come help with the party? He knows nothing about Hemingway, but he makes a mean drink and can generally just help wherever you need an extra hand. LMK!

Felicity: Oh and what's the dress code? Are we doing like casual? Fancy? Somewhere in between? I'm not one to hang around with academic types.

I saw her texts when I got out of the shower. She wanted to come and help with the party? I assumed Edwin didn't mention to her our blow up the night before.

Me: You don't have to spend your vacation schlepping drinks and hors d'oeuvres

Felicity: Trust me. There's nowhere I'd rather be. Klaus too. We love everything about Candy Cane Key, and if this is the night's activity, we're all in! Plus, I want to hang out and hear how your date went. 😊

Me: The party starts at five. We'll probably be ready and assembled at four just in case people show up early. I'm about to head over now just so I can start thawing the prepared foods and getting things ready for tonight.

Felicity: Cool. We'll be over around lunch. I have so much to tell you! And I have the skinny about Marley and Asher too, in case he's super tight lipped when he sees you.

IN ALL THE melodrama of the night I'd forgotten about Asher and Marley. Maybe my gossip would slip from everyone's notice with everyone focused on his love child's sudden appearance. On my front stoop sat a vase filled with passion flower and acacia. I didn't even have to read the card to know who sent them. And the subtle meaning behind the selection was not lost on me either. Both the passion flower and the acacia buds attracted the Acacia Blue butterfly. Edwin got an A+ for effort that was for sure. It would have been quite a feat to find them in the meadow and pick enough for a vaseful.

A woman like you is the rarest treasure. - Edwin

He left a p.s. on the back of the card.

P.S. - this pirate appreciates that booty too.

WELL PLAYED, Wheeler, I thought with a chuckle. I tucked the card in my pocket, and placed the flowers on my kitchen counter. Maybe it wouldn't be such a bad day after all.

"HOLY CRAP!" Felicity bound into the pub, dress slung over her shoulder, Klaus following behind her as she beelined straight for me. "This place looks freaking amazing! You guys did so much more after I left yesterday!"

I took her around and walked her through the evening's event. From who was speaking when, what passages we planned to read, and our video that made me both excited and nauseous with worry over it malfunctioning.

"While I know my cousin put you up to it," Klaus held out his fist when Felicity and I made it back to the bar, pounding it against mine when I caught on he wanted to compliment me. "Well played. Felicity and I laughed for probably the rest of the night thinking about those two signs."

"Speaking of." Felicity popped up and looked around, I assumed trying to place Edwin. "Where is everyone?"

I pointed to all of my crew working hard on various

projects. Of all the years that we'd had this event, this was the calmest and most organized we'd probably ever been. I hadn't even had to screech the time at anyone like some banshee counting down to imminent demise.

"I mean, no Edwin. No Asher? Marley and Bear? I thought for sure they'd all be here, and we could all get the gossip concurrently."

No one in the room even flinched at the word gossip. Surely someone had to have heard about me and Edwin.

"What happened to you guys last night?" Klaus asked. "When we came back around on the boat, we looked for you, and you were gone. And you weren't at MariJo's or at Edwin's place —no one was home when the Master of Ceremonies dropped us off in his golf cart."

"Did Edwin give you a taste of his *candy cane* back at your place?" Felicity nudged me with her elbow with an exaggerated wink.

I watched my staff with an eagle eye. Not a single one of them cared about our conversation. No one stopped in their tracks or looked at me nervously, none of the typical signs of town gossip.

"No," I told them. "We packed up after the fireworks were over. Edwin was worried that I wouldn't get enough sleep to handle the big day today. I haven't seen him since about ten o'clock last night."

Felicity grabbed me by the hand and pulled me toward a banquette.

"Okay, I need all the skinny. You guys are dating, right? Because I don't want to embarrass you. Let's just say we know you spent the night at his house. And well, y'all weren't quiet. But Edwin is so damn tightlipped about everything. And MariJo is just like 'you leave those two alone, they've been tap dancing around one another in the world's slowest mating ritual known to man!' And I was like 'damn girl, that was savage!' But also... you're together now, right?"

There was so much to dissect. MariJo thought we'd been tap dancing around one another? Somehow I didn't know how to process that. She'd never made mention of the fact that Edwin was interested in me. And we'd known one another for years now given we were both on the Christmas committee. The rest I chose to ignore for my own still reeling sense of mortification.

"God, you're as bad as him." She threw her hands up in mock frustration. "Just tell me he gave you a good dicking. Because I would hate to be proven a liar if he's super shitty in bed after I oversold the hell out of his skills."

Where was a drink when you needed one? I looked over my shoulder, hoping to draw the attention of literally anyone authorized to go behind the bar and grab me a beer. Or a straight shot of vodka. Anything to put me out of the soul shrinking misery of discussing just how good I'd been *dicked* by Edwin Wheeler.

"Our status isn't solidified," I replied, in an attempt to find the most neutral ground to stay on. After yelling at him the night before about being the gossip around town, the last thing I wanted to do was to be the source of gossip about the two of us.

"Bullshit. You're flushed clear up to your hairline. I don't know what it is about the two of you. We're family. Klaus and Edwin are practically brothers which means you and me are practically sisters. And sisters give the skinny about the lady earthquakes that our talented men provide. But, if you're gonna be all tightlipped and shy—fine. That's your prerogative."

She shrugged, airily tossing out her objections as if she wasn't dying to get any information.

Thankfully I was saved from having to verify anything by the appearance of the very man that we'd just been discussing.

"Where are your storm shutters?" Edwin asked, in place of a hello.

"My storm shutters?" I asked, my brain struggling to quickly switch topics from Felicity begging for tawdry details of my sex life, to Edwin's no nonsense need to fix something on my bar.

"Yes, those white pieces of wood that you hang from the beams outside and tie down in an effort to protect the bar in the event large gusts of wind threaten to blow you clear off the island."

I launched out of the booth, hot on his heels as he stomped through the seating area and pushed through my kitchen toward my storage shed out back.

"What are you doing?" I asked as he threw the doors open and started pulling them out one by one.

"What does it look like?" he asked, looking at me as if I'd just asked him what color the sky was—which incidentally looked a menacing gray. We were definitely in for that rain storm the weather guys had been talking about. "I'm putting up your storm shutters."

"I see that." I folded my arms beneath my chest, feeling my core temperature rise at his insolence. "*Why* are you putting up my storm shutters?"

With a huff, he dropped the piece of wood, balancing it against his shoulder. He turned and pointed with an aggressive frown toward the giant, gray black clouds rolling toward us from the horizon. "Do you see that storm? It's coming this way."

"You always make fun of me for putting up those shutters," I told him, trying to take the piece of wood from his hands and place it back in my storage closet. "Why suddenly change tactics now?"

The wind kicked up at that very moment, as if in cahoots with Edwin to make sure they both succumbed to the panic the weathermen liked to force on the island for ratings.

"Acacia, not now. I need to get these up, immediately."

"No." I held on to the other side. "Not until you tell me why after years of making fun of me, treating me like I'm the asshole for wanting to protect my place of business, would you suddenly come running out here with your hands up screaming in terror over a few drops of rain."

He pressed the shutter back against the closet, frustration making his arms flex and his jaw tick. I watched him take three deep breaths and count as he exhaled. It didn't take more than five seconds, yet it felt as if it stretched on for eternity. I'd never seen him that agitated, especially not directed toward me. I wondered offhand if it was because I was such a jerk the night before.

"Look, if this is about last night…" I hedged.

"Jesus Christ! Acacia—look at the clouds. There is a named tropical storm heading this way. They think it might strengthen into a hurricane by the time it hits the Keys. You need to get your storm shutters up right now."

He tried to maneuver around me, but there was nowhere for him to go. And I was not done with my questions. I needed more information than just whatever Mr.

Overbearing deigned to throw my way in the midst of a tornado of activity.

"No."

I pressed my hand to his chest. I felt him shiver beneath his shirt. The heat of his chest against the cool of my fingers sent a warm wave of longing through my bloodstream as well.

"Acacia." He forced through gritted teeth. "We need to get a move on."

"Absolutely not. You put those storm shutters up, and you'll scare off all of the people coming to my event. They'll think it's canceled, and it will be ruined. We don't need the storm shutters. You always say they're blowing smoke up our asses, and it will be a few droplets of rain, and then we'll all look like morons falling for it again."

We'd acquired an audience. Klaus and Felicity stood at the back door, watching us go back and forth. My head cook and several of the line chefs joined us on the grass and were trying to sneak around Edwin to help pull shutters out. Those traitors. Who were they to take Edwin's side?

"Acacia, all of those beautiful picture windows, the ones that you can open and close so people can take in the sea breeze on picture perfect days—they cost a small fortune to install. I remember when you put them in. You told Charlie and Hank that they'd pay off when people flocked to your little inlet to sit at your bar and just bask in the glory of gorgeous sunsets and postcard-worthy ocean views. Do you remember?"

He gathered the hand that was pressing against his chest and cradled it against his face. His lips pressed against my pulse point, unspooling long ribbons of desire up my arm and through my nervous system.

"Can you imagine what a horrible loss it would be if the wind from the storm shattered them? And what happens if you're at the bar, laughing and talking to party goers when that gust of wind hits? I'd never forgive myself if you got hurt over something that could have been easily prevented by these pieces of wood. Let us put them up? Okay? Just to be safe. If the storm blows over, well—I'll let you decide what to do with me."

He smirked a devil may care smile at me and winked. He already knew he'd won. I didn't even put up a fight as he pulled the piece of wood out from beneath my other hand and set to getting them all hung.

WITH EVERY PASSING hour the sky got darker. And with each update of the proximity of the storm to us, Acacia dug her heels in deeper. Thankfully my mom and most of the elderly ladies of the island had taken heed that morning and evacuated toward the mainland just to be safe. The storm wasn't expected to be massive, a Cat One at most, but any suggestion of a powerful storm needed to be taken seriously.

Klaus and I quietly had let Acacia's staff go home so they could take care of storm proofing their own houses and getting to their families. Everyone knew what Acacia refused to acknowledge. There would be no party. Mother Nature had other plans. Temperance had, however, become the gathering place for a few of us with nowhere else to go. Felicity practically vibrated with excitement, mentioning every thirty minutes or so that she'd always wanted to experience a hurricane.

Asher, Marley, and her husband Bear arrived some time

ago, and we were all seated in a horseshoe booth along with Felicity and Klaus. Asher had regaled them all with hours of stories about his years at Dartmouth and the Shakespeare festival. They'd moved on to Marley's recounting of giving birth to her twins two years ago at that very festival where she'd gone in search of Asher.

Now faced with the hurricane, she turned to Bear every so often to tell him she wished that they wouldn't have come, and that she worried if their kids would be okay with someone named Raven and Penn if something happened to them.

"The word hurricane sounds scary," I told them, interrupting their conversation. "But more than likely this will stay a tropical storm, which is probably akin to a really bad thunderstorm. If it bumps up to a Cat One, it will be a really bad thunderstorm with some scary sounding wind. But we'll be okay. Most of the danger will be from falling trees, or from the tide getting pushed up against the breakers. Since we're in an inlet, we'll be safe from the worst of the tidewaters, and we're in a steel building so the chances of a tree doing any damage are minimal. We'll be just fine."

They all seemed to take comfort in what I said, returning to their stories about theaters, plays, and the old Bard— which was apparently Shakespeare's nickname. They couldn't hold my attention. Not when Acacia wore a path in her wood floors, pacing back and forth from the windows to the door, and back again.

"Acacia," I gathered her shoulders in my hands, trying to hold her still and quiet her nervous energy. "I need you to listen to me."

She refused to meet my eyes. Even when I took her chin between my fingers and tilted her face up. Stubbornly she tilted her eyes toward the door, as if any moment a rush of people would come rushing in bemoaning the high winds and potential thunderstorm.

"They aren't coming, sweetheart." I pressed my lips to her forehead, as if that single act would take away all of her disappointment.

"Of course, they're going to come. It's Hemingway's one hundred and twenty-fifth birthday. It's too important to miss. We have a video this year—and we changed the whole program because you thought it was boring and needed to be refreshed. Asher worked so hard on getting all of the details just so. It's going to happen. Maybe people will be a little delayed because traffic always gums up when there's a rainstorm, but they'll be here any minute now and we need to be ready."

"Sweetheart," I tried again. "Look at me. Please."

Reluctantly those hydrangea hued eyes met mine, and my heart sank. There was a storm of emotions gathering, and none of those emotions were pleasant.

"I want nothing more than for you to have the very best party you've ever thrown. I want the whole town here, plus all the famous literary greats. In fact, we'll reschedule and the whole town will shout it from the rooftops to ensure Hemingway gets a proper one hundred and twenty fifth celebration. But right now? Today? No one is coming. They issued an evacuation alert an hour ago. The storm is two hours away."

A giant clap of thunder drew surprised squeaks from both Marley and Felicity.

"Did you hear that?" I asked her. Though she'd have to

have been deaf to miss it. It's too dangerous for anyone to be out there right now. The news channels are all saying if people haven't evacuated by now, they'll need to shelter in place now until it passes."

"Are we really going to be okay?" Marley asked, with that glassy eyed look that usually meant she was on the verge of tears.

"It's going to be fine, princess." Her husband cradled her against his chest. "It's just a little rain. Look, even if it does get upgraded to a Category One hurricane, the videos on YouTube just show some wind blowing trees around and some shingles falling off. We've had worse than that in Chicago, right?"

That appeared to ease the worst of her anxiety.

"What do you say we break into some of this food?" Asher suggested. "It's all been heated now so it can't be refrozen, so it will go to waste. We may as well all enjoy a nice dinner while we wait out the storm."

TROPICAL STORM ALPHA slammed into the Keys with a vengeance. The storm sirens had been going off for the better part of an hour, grating everyone's nerves raw. According to the National Weather Service, the storm had just begun to encroach on the Keys but already they were concerned that with all the warm water in the ocean, the storm would grow as it made landfall.

The rain felt as if it hit the bar sideways in rapid, machine gun bursts of moisture that rattled the glass and ping ponged off the steel roof. The effects were so loud it deafened one's ears and almost tilted your equilibrium.

We still had service on our phones, and thankfully enough of the staff had backup chargers they left at work that all of us were fully powered for now. Eventually, the power would go out. It was just the nature of these storms. We had our backup flashlights and lanterns at the ready. Acacia and her team had moved everyone into one of the larger storage closets.

"It sounds really bad out there," Felicity said to Klaus.

"Temperance was built with steel," I explained. "It sounds bad because the whole structure is metal. It pings. But better to ping and make noise than to quietly get torn apart."

The wind gusts got stronger, and we heard something hit the side of the building. While there were boats in some of the marinas further up the inlet, my guess was it was something smaller that had been light enough to get tossed by the storm. Perhaps a grill, or a fiberglass boat cover.

"Bear, I'm really scared." Marley pressed herself into her husband, accepting the comfort of his arms.

"It's going to be okay, Marley," Asher assured her. "Why don't you tell me more about your mom. I want to know everything about Joy while you were growing up."

That drew an excited smile from her, and she dove in enthusiastically chatting to Asher about her life in a tiny town called North Pole, New York—where incidentally they *also* celebrated Christmas all year round. Felicity and Klaus hung on their every word, making quiet plans to go up and stay at Marley's bed and breakfast.

The alarms rang out again, screeching their warning that the first band of Tropical Storm Alpha was passing overhead. Acacia had been puttering back and forth in the storage room, making sure everyone had supplies within reach. When the new alarm sounded, she jumped, practically falling into my arms.

"They always threaten that tropical storms and hurricanes are imminent, but this is the first time they were actually right."

I felt her tremble. Every instinct told me to protect but there was nothing I could do against the fear of the unknown and nature. But I could be her source of comfort.

"Remember two summers ago, there was that huge thunderstorm right before the Fourth of July? And you were out in the rain, stomping around in galoshes and a rain jacket, crawling underneath the docks looking for Six-Toed Joe?"

Everyone else in the room was listening to Bear and Marley discuss the year they met each other in North Pole. The two of them were such complete opposites yet watching them smile at one another made me desperate to have what they did.

"He'd somehow slipped out the back door," Acacia laughed. "And I was worried he'd get spooked by all the thunder and end up lost or swept out to sea."

"How did you come by Six-Toed Joe?" Asher asked, bouncing his focus between the two conversations.

"He found me." Acacia shrugged, pulling the cat into her lap and nuzzling into his scruff. "The day I got the keys for the bar I was sitting there, wondering what the hell I'd done to myself buying this place and mulishly convincing myself I could handle it. I'd been looking under the bar, trying to figure out how to turn on the main water valve, and there he was —a little black and white fluff ball curled up in the back corner of the cabinet. When I saw his mitten paws..." she held up his front paws to show off his extra 'thumbs,' "I thought it had to be a sign. Someone who came to Candy Cane Key to open a Hemingway bar finds a cat with mitten paws? What are the odds? Six-Toed Joe became the official mascot of Temperance. He even has his own Instagram page and a merchandise line."

That surprised me. She truly did have great business instincts. And naturally an adorable cat with mittens for paws and a mustache that made him look like his name should be Mario—he probably didn't just have a just page on the internet. He more than likely dominated the social media platform. He was a cute cat. Even me, the non-cat person, had a soft spot for him.

Something heavy and fragile crashed against the side of the building, the sound of shattering glass and splintering wood ricocheted all around us just as the power dropped us into the pitch black. Marley screamed, Felicity started to cry, but Acacia set about crawling around by our feet, turning each of our emergency lamps on one by one.

Even with the three lamps combined, they cast a weak glow around us.

"We may need to conserve those," I told Acacia but loud enough for the group to hear. "It's not even seven o'clock. We have a lot of hours in the dark before the storm passes and these lamps have seen better days."

"What if we just use one at a time?" Felicity asked, her voice trembling with emotion. "I don't know if I want to be completely in the dark."

Asher and Bear turned two of the three lamps off, reducing the ring around us.

"We still have our cell phones, too." Klaus held his up,

engaging his flashlight. "Not for continuous use," he clarified. "But in a pinch—if we need to go use the restroom or there's a reason to go back into the main dining area— just a reminder you have the use of your phone too."

Something else heavy crashed into the side of the building.

"It can't possibly be the eyewall?" I asked, though I realized quickly I was the most experienced among the group. We'd sent all of Acacia's staff home before the storm started.

"What's an eye wall?" Felicity asked Klaus, as if he'd know. Rather than answer he pointed toward me.

"It's the back half of a hurricane. Typically, it's more powerful than the front half because of the centrifugal force of the wind whipping around in a circular pattern. That tends to be when things really get damaged. But the storm just made landfall, so I can't imagine that it is the eye wall already."

"We're going to die," Felicity cried. "If we haven't even hit the eye wall yet, and already the outside is threatening to bring down this building, we have no hope."

I tried to tell her, once again, that we hadn't even reached hurricane levels yet, and we weren't in any real danger, but Felicity wanted none of what I told her.

"When you are with your mom," Acacia wrapped her arm through mine resting her head on my bicep. "You always repeat whatever someone says, loud enough that she can catch it with her good ear. But you do it in such a way that it looks like you're talking to whomever just spoke while also giving your mom the dignity of not having to ask to repeat what was said."

Her words were barely a whisper. No one else would be

able to hear her, especially not over Felicity's melodramatic wailing about all the things she wouldn't get to do in her life.

"You hire Manny to take care of small repairs, even though I've seen you do the same kinds of things with your eyes closed."

He was a good friend. And sometimes business was slow. Especially during the off season.

"When you think no one is looking, you throw pieces of fish at Six-Toed Joe. The good pieces, too. The stuff that the fishing boats leave for others to use as bait the next time they take fishermen out on tour."

Where the two of us sat nearest the door was too far from the main circle of our friends for the weak lamplight to reach us. We were as close to bathed in darkness as the room would reach. Acacia took that opportunity to throw her leg over my thigh and settle herself in my lap, so we were nose to nose.

"If this hurricane is going to kill us," she chuckled.

"Tropical storm," I corrected.

"If today is my last night on earth, I have a confession to make."

My heart raced as if I'd just run a marathon. The feel of her hands against my cheeks bathed me in tenderness that had my hands twitching to gather her in my arms and kiss the sense back into her.

"What?" I asked.

Her fingers scratched up along my five o'clock shadow, her cheek rested against mine, the gentle whisper of her breath tickled against my ear lobe.

"I'm the one who volunteered you for the Manuary auction, not your mom."

There wasn't even a word to describe the emotions that rushed through me. She had executed the world's most perfect checkmate, and I never even knew it was her. That little brat.

"What?" I laughed, the shock making the statement come out louder than I thought it would. "Why on earth would you do that?"

"Why on earth would you do what?" Klaus asked.

"There is this auction," I explained, tempering my voice to within a normal range so no one looked too closely at our position.

I loved having Acacia in my lap. The last thing I wanted was her to spook and leave. My arms tightened around her back, hoping she understood how badly I wanted her to stay there.

"We have an auction here every January. It raises money for conservation. This year it was to save the spotted deer. Ms. Ashley, over here, just admitted that it wasn't my *mother* who secretly put my name on the auction sheet. It was *her*."

I tugged at her hair, finding her neck with my lips in the dark, and taking a long, suckling bite from that tendon knowing it would drive her wild.

"I just don't know why she would."

"Because I know how much you *hate* it. And it was fun to watch you get all riled up year after year as you got called to the stage and auctioned off like the prized steer at the 4H."

The whole room erupted into hysterics at my expense. At least their laughter hid the sound of the storm battering against the walls of Acacia's building.

"You should have seen how pissed he was," Acacia tried to tell them through gasping laughter. "He could have spit nails clear across the room had he had them. Stomping up onto the stage, staring down every woman in the room. All those nice old ladies with their fifty-dollar bids were too intimidated to even volley an opening."

It wasn't nearly as bad as she made it out to be. I had been annoyed. My mom, naturally, attended the auction as part of all things Candy Cane Key, but I thought I was simply her escort. I'd been totally blindsided on my participation.

"Did anyone bid on you?" Klaus asked, equally invested in the story.

I shrugged, then realized he couldn't see me in the shadows.

"Someone did. But it was an anonymous bid, and they never even collected on their date."

Acacia squirmed in my lap. Her ass rubbing against my thighs, as if she anticipated getting a swat across those luscious swells. I'd always suspected. Though everyone had been so tightlipped about the bidder and their donation. They'd told me the bidder didn't want anything from me. Rather, they saw how uncomfortable I looked onstage and they'd submitted the max bid simply so I'd be freed from being on stage.

At the time I thought nothing of it. I'd simply been grateful to make a quick exit. But now, feeling Acacia in my lap, and knowing she was the one that put me up there— the pieces all fell into place.

"So I owe you a date then, I guess?" I whispered into her ear.

I felt her shoulder tilt up, sensed the smile spreading across her lips.

"We had a pretty great one already. I'd say that your tab is wiped clean."

"And yet, there is the little issue of evening the score." I nip at her earlobe. "I'd say that offering me up like a prized side of beef definitely makes you *very* naughty. If you were mine...I don't know if I could let that level of naughtiness go unnoticed."

I dipped my toe into the waters, hoping she'd take the bait of my little test.

"I'm already yours, Edwin."

Her arms snaked around my neck, and her lips came down on mine in the most gentle kiss.

"That's what I'm doing a terrible job trying to tell you. I put you up there because I knew you'd hate it. But then, the more I saw how uncomfortable you were up there, the less I enjoyed making you squirm. I pulled you down because, well, I didn't like seeing you suffer. It actually really bothered me.

"Yesterday, I was afraid I'd be forced to admit how much I loved you, too. Before I was ready. Because all this time, I didn't realize that the reason it was so easy for you to get a rise out of me was because I actually cared about what you thought about me. I wanted you to like me, and every time you poked fun at me—it felt like you were rejecting me."

There were a host of words that she'd said in that monologue while sitting on my lap. But it was a single sentence that replayed in my head on repeat. She loved me? It had to have been intentional. After all the b.s. and the petty back and forth, her coming to that realization while she sat on my lap and listed all the small things she noticed about me—just as I'd done to her a few days prior...it couldn't be a coincidence.

"Acacia?" I asked. "Do you realize what you just said?"

"I love you, Edwin." I felt her face directly in front of

mine as she said it. "I didn't realize it. Not right away, anyway. But it's been there, slowly taking root over the years until I just couldn't ignore it anymore. And well, since we might be dying tonight," she learned forward and buried her face in my neck. "I figured I may as well unburden my soul while I still can."

Acacia

INTELLECTUALLY, I knew that we were perfectly safe. Even huddled in that tiny storage closet with the tiniest beams of light, and the shrieks and cries of all of my friends drowning out the noise of the storm, I had zero doubts about our safety.

But damn, high winds, crashing waves, and the incessant drone of emergency sirens did exactly as one would expect– Scared the living shit out of you. Every clank, crash, and boom set my teeth on edge. Even with Edwin cradling me against his chest, whispering comforting words in my ear, I still shook with an excess of adrenaline.

When we heard the power transformer snap, then pop, and sizzle just outside my pub, the images that haunted my imagination had me cowering with consuming fear.

"I want to get married, Klaus," Felicity called into the darkness; the battery having died on one of three lanterns already. "Right now. I want to know that if anything happens to one of us between now and when the storm ends that we're married."

It didn't seem right to remind them that without a marriage certificate obtained and filed three days prior to the wedding, any vows exchanged wouldn't be valid.

"I'm ordained!" Asher cried triumphantly. "I can marry you right now if you want."

I could hear everyone readjusting in their seats around me. Both of the lamps went on, causing all of us to smart against the dim light. Felicity shuffled on her knees over to Klaus, removing every last centimeter of space between the two of them.

"I've never been more out of my head than I am right now, Klaus. But the one thing I know. The one thing I've known every single day since you went outside in a blizzard and made me a birthday cake out of snow, is that no one can calm me, bring me peace, hold me up, or stand proudly next to me like you. It has always been you. Even as we navigated life before we met—there was always a place carved out in the universe where we were destined to be together. This crazy week has shown me that I never laugh harder than when I'm with you. My smiles are bigger, my joy is fuller, and every single day I spend next to you is a day fully lived and loved. I want to be your wife today, tomorrow, and fifty years from now. And when we look back on our lives, when we're old and crotchety, I know I won't have a single regret for the life I lived with you. You are my favorite human, and I'll spend my whole life showing you how deeply I love you, and how proud I am to be your wife."

There was a hush across the whole room. It felt as if even the storm had paused to hear Felicity pledge her love to Klaus. We all collectively held our breath while we waited for Klaus to begin.

"I love you," Klaus murmured, emotion clogging his

voice. "When I met you, I was at the lowest point of my life, Princess. Love was the foulest four-letter word. I'd resigned myself to living alone for the remainder of however many years I had left. Slowly losing sight of any wisp of joy until you came waltzing into my bathroom pointing those pretty little nails at me and accusing *me* of breaking into your AirBnb. After my first marriage collapsed, I never thought I'd fall in love again, and I certainly never expected it to blindside me. But since that day, I've lived more in these two years than in a lifetime before you. You inspire me, challenge me to be a better person every single day. You love unconditionally and fearlessly, and you are ferociously in my corner always. The words *I love you* don't fit the breadth of emotion I have for you, my Christmas angel. But I will spend every day for the rest of my life ensuring you know just how deeply my love for you goes."

Asher looked to both of them, clapping his hands as if witnessing the world's best performance and announced, "by the State of Florida and the powers vested in me, I declare Felicity Miller and Klaus Baer married before these witnesses and apparently the heavens that are presently baptizing you in new love, and hopefully, the impending end to this storm."

As if the storm agreed, the sky seemed to be split in two under the most capricious clap of thunder we'd heard to that point. It was so strong and so violent, we felt the walls shake. Though Felicity and Klaus didn't seem to notice.

I STARTLED AWAKE, disorientated in the pitch black. I heard the deep rumble of Six-Toed Joe's purr somewhere at my back, and the random, ambient sounds of others sleeping around me. It slowly came back to me. The storm, the wedding, retreating to the storage closet to keep away from any potential projectiles.

The space to my right was empty. The place where he'd been felt cold as if he'd gotten up a while ago and never returned. I grabbed my cell phone, and as carefully as I could snuck out of the storage room in search of Edwin.

"Hey." He called to me as soon as I closed the door behind me. "What are you doing awake?"

He sat at a booth near the back of the bar. The power was still off, none of the ambient hums of the refrigerators could be heard. I could barely make him out sitting in that booth, if not for the slightest peek of moonlight that had winnowed its way between two of the storm shutters.

The tables and such were still set up for the party that didn't happen. Not that I expected a magic fairy to have come while I slept and cleaned. But in all that had happened in the last few hours, I'd practically forgotten we'd been in the midst of trying to host a party.

I tried not to mourn that fact. There would be other Hemingway Days. And the important part was everyone was safe, and we rode out the storm. I could still hear it outside, though it was mostly just heavy rain and the occasional rumble of thunder.

"I woke up, and you weren't there," I told him. "So I decided to see what you've gotten into out here. Not nipping at my top shelf shit, are you? Because Taffy measures it with a digital leveler."

He extended his hand, and I went to him, linking our fingers together.

"I was thinking about Klaus and Felicity," his voice was lullaby soft as he ran his lips across my knuckles. "Something Klaus said—about how quickly he fell for her. And I've been sitting here trying to figure out when exactly that was for me. Is love a quieter kind of falling when you've known someone so long? Is it different from someone like Klaus and Felicity who knew their clock was ticking because they were on vacation?"

I wondered offhand what time it was. Without a clock, or even seeing how dark it was outside, there was no way to tell if it was the middle of the night or almost morning. Then I realized I held my phone in my hands, which was equipped with a clock. Three fifteen.

"But if we love each other, does it matter when it happened?"

"I care about you too much to hurt you, Acacia. I just want to make sure."

"That's love, Edwin." That realization felt like the first sunbeam breaking through those storm clouds. "Like I said last night about pulling you down off the auction block. I couldn't watch you in any form of pain. Because *I love you*. And it took this—" I gestured between the pair of us, "whatever we're calling it, to realize that it was never about hating you. It was about slowly realizing I loved you, and being scared to get hurt if you didn't love me back."

Edwin held me tight against him, pressing his lips to my cheek and holding me. We sat in contemplative silence for long moments, listening to the tapering storm. Eventually, he swung his legs around, helping me slide off his body and next to him on the seat.

"So what do we do now?" he asked, gathering my hair in his hand, twisting it, and arranging it behind my shoulder.

"Right now, this very minute or now, in the sense that we've laid down our swords and are no longer adversaries but allies?"

I could see very little of him in the dark. But I caught his shadow as he threw his head back, letting out an entertained chuckle. The sound of it is the most soothing balm after a night of anxiety.

"I was thinking now that I know you love me, and I love you—and we're too damn old to square dance around being together with one another. I want you, Acacia. Forever. Believe me, I'm far more romantic than a pitch-black proposal three days after we had sex for the first time, but I also know you're it for me. I'm a simple man, and I know what I want. And what I want is you. Forever."

I saw our life tumble out in front of me. Him with his boat tours, gratuitously flirting with me as he drove by every day, our nights filled with friends and books, and picnics on our knoll. Felicity had been right all along. She was going to be my family now. Something I found I looked forward to.

"And what about right this very minute?" I asked, hoping my voice sounded as seductive as I imagined it would.

"What did you have in mind, Sweet Acacia?"

Edwin's hand went up my dress, running his fingers up and down the backs of my thighs.

"Well...we called parlay. We met and discussed the terms of our truce. But typically the host of the negotiations offers a gift as a show of good faith to their adversary."

"Funny, I don't remember reading about that in my pirate books."

His fingers stretched from where they gripped my thighs, the tips grazing along my slit, sending a shiver straight up my spine.

"Oh, yes," I invoked my professorial tone, forcing my voice to stay firm and sure. "It's a very well-known tradition. You must have been sick the day they taught it."

"That's very possible. I did attend a lot of parties at that plebeian institution of mine." He chuckled, hooking his fingers into the gusset of my panties, using the back of his knuckle to kiss at my clit. "What does this well known, good faith parlay gift entail?"

"I think that it's usually something equally beneficial for both parties. For example...what if you took me over to that bar." I nodded over my shoulder in the dark. "Bend me over, raise your mast..."

I fisted my hand into his hair. It had to be all the adrenaline from the storm, the fighting, and knowing he harbored a secret kink for pirates—whatever it was, I wanted to give him everything he wanted.

"...and plunder me."

I barely got the words out, and I was swept, basket style, in his arms. The cool wood of the bar felt delicious against my overheated skin. Edwin rolled up my dress, barely past my hips, and pressed his fingers into my pussy as far as they would go.

"You just unlocked Pandora's box, sweet thing,." he told me, running his fingers through my slit, lighting up my whole body with electricity.

"Give me your worst." I tried to growl, biting my lip in an attempt not to laugh. I'd wanted to say more. To call him the Dread Pirate Wheeler, but I couldn't hold a straight face let alone say a full sentence.

"I have no condoms, Acacia." He continued to fuck his fingers into me, twisting them and glancing against my g-spot.

"I trust you," I told him. "It's a small town. We know each other's business. Hell, we see the same doctor, so you know I'm in the on the regular getting my birth control shots. So."

I circled my hips in the air, humming with delight against the friction his fingers created.

"What do you say, Dread Pirate Wheeler...are you going to claim what's yours? I believe according to the card you sent me...you like my booty. Prove it."

It was as if I'd unleashed a rabid dog and given him the attack order. Edwin's hand covered my mouth as he thrust into me. He set a bruising pace. My nerve endings spit and sputtered, desire swirled deep in my core, while my brain uselessly grasped at every piece of stimuli, unsure which to hang on to and which to discard.

The slap of his skin against mine beat in tandem with the rain droplets hitting the roof. Our attempts to stay quiet as we fought against our conclusions with each slide of his cock in and out of my body. My bruised nipples were getting pressed and pulled against the wood of the bar. Yet everything Edwin did, every tawdry whisper in my ear juxtaposed against each gentle kiss and sweet caress, bound us in an energy that pressed with desperation to be released.

"I don't think I can be quiet," I warned, when his hand moved from in front of my mouth to wrap around my hair and pull it taut.

"It's your choice, sweets," he chuckled. "Since you were so worried about two old ladies knowing we were doing this exact thing yesterday—by all means, scream into the rafters.

Wake up the whole group. Hearing you scream my name, mindless with pleasure, would have me proudly beating my chest and strutting like a peacock."

I bit against my lips, feeling my orgasm slowly build. This one wasn't going to be a freight train, it would be a volcano that took out everything in its path. We were lost. Mindless with passion. My body ached but also felt as if only a run at full speed could soothe my coiling muscles. I needed to come but wanted it to go on forever. I wanted to lay down and watch Edwin's beautiful face contort with every tendril of pleasure he luxuriated in. But, I needed him desperately to hold me down and use me.

"We have forever." I promised him, as if he could hear all of my warring thoughts. "Today, tomorrow, next week, next month—for years and years."

I felt him thickening. His pace picked up, his hips ground against mine in a seductive dance.

"I love you, Acacia." He murmured into my ear, as his fingers found my clit and the two of us tumbled into a dual completion, "Earnestly.

Twenty~Three

EDWIN

EIGHT MONTHS LATER

Tropical Storm Alpha did a number on our little Key. While there wasn't any significant damage, no one got hurt, and no businesses were destroyed—it sure left behind one hell of a mess. Mud, downed trees, garbage and debris strewn about. It took the Key a good while to set ourselves back to rights. But that was one of the best parts of living in Candy Cane Key. You always had a friend in your neighbors. We all pitched in, and by August, the Key looked as good as new. Unfortunately for Acacia, she didn't get to celebrate Hemingway's birthday as she wanted. I know even though she put on a brave face, it disappointed her. Deeply.

"Where are you two taking me?" she grumbled, trying to pull at the blindfold that Felicity insisted we use.

Felicity and Klaus, after saying their vows in the middle of that storm, decided to make it really legal a few days later at the Candy Cane Key Courthouse. Though, they did have to have another pretend wedding for Felicity's because in *her* words, her sister was "all in her feelings" that Acacia got to be her maid of honor.

"Can you just chill for like five minutes of your life?" Felicity teased her. "You are in good hands, little control freak."

We led her into WCCK's radio station, where Bear and his crew waited for her alongside a very special guest.

"Friends of the Bear and Raven morning show, we have a very special edition of our show this morning. We're broadcasting live from the studios in Candy Cane Key, the home of our good friends Edwin Wheeler and Acacia Ashley—soon to be Wheeler—who as you may remember were our gracious hosts, and our greatest comfort last summer while we braved a tropical storm."

"You know, Marley still hasn't stopped talking about her near-death experience, Bear. Perhaps bringing her back down here wasn't the best idea." His co-host Raven chimed in.

Acacia was perched on one of the studio chairs, still blindfolded, and seated next to someone who, once she took off her blindfold and saw who it was, she'd absolutely lose her shit. And I stood at the ready, iPhone already recording because I wanted to relive this moment over and over again.

"Those out in radio-land can't see—because we aren't live-streaming today—our friend Acacia is seated with a blindfold on. She has no idea who is sitting directly next to her, whom we've been speaking with for the last ten minutes. Mystery guest, would you like to tell Acacia why you're here?"

Acacia went to relieve herself of the blindfold. Felicity stayed her hand, whispering in her ear that Bear lived for dramatic reveals and to sit tight for just two more seconds. A directive that my lovely soon- to- be wife did not appreciate.

"Ms. Ashley, we meet again." The mystery guest spoke into the microphone but was turned toward Acacia. "You have a lot of people here who love and respect you. They think the world of you. A few of them reached out on your behalf to my offices."

Thank god Felicity's friends chose the week of Christmas in July to come down and pay a visit to "Grandpa Krane", as he was now called in their house. If not for Bear and his ability to track down practically anyone and call in a favor— I would not have been able to give my soon-to-be-bride-in two days, the ultimate wedding gift.

"In recognition of your wedding, and of all the work you have done over the years to further the legacy of my grandfather, Ernest Hemingway, I am officially declaring you a member of the Ernest Hemingway Society with full academic rights and recognitions."

Acacia was sobbing before the blindfold even came off her face. I may have shed a tear or two seeing such unfettered joy and surprise on her face. Who was I kidding? I was a blubbering fucking mess.

After thanking the Hemingway family member—whose name I didn't catch—and thanking everyone who made it possible she turned to me, holding up the very official looking leather binder.

"You did this for me?" she cried, her fancy painted wedding nails covering her lips. "I can't believe you did this. For me."

"Sweet Acacia," I drew her in against my chest, rubbing her back as she cried her joy and surprise into my neck, "I will move mountains to ensure every day, you know that my world is meaningless without you in it."

"...and there you have it, folks." Bear exclaimed into the microphone. "From enemies in earnest to earnestly in love... I want to be the first to congratulate the soon to be Mr. and Mrs. Wheeler on a joy-filled wedding and a life filled with love."

"Just one small point of clarification, my friend."

I pulled Acacia into my side, her eyes rounding with surprise and concern. Though I knew what she was afraid of, I wouldn't tell a soul that I'd put a baby in her roughly six weeks ago. That was our secret. For now anyway. Hopefully no one noticed her drinking sparkling cider at the wedding.

"That would be *Dr.* and Mr. Wheeler," I clarified. "She's worked hard to earn the title."

Our lives look a bit different these days. *Three Sheets Charters* experienced a bit of a pivot. While we still offered a libation or two on our ship, our tours were less *Girls Gone Wild* and more a highlight of the rich history of our fabulous Key. *From Pirates to Poets* now featured contributions and readings not just from me, but both Acacia and Grandpa Krane—when he wasn't in Chicago visiting his grandkids— hopped the tours with me to offer expanded insight.

Klaus and Felicity visited regularly. So much so that they now shared my side of the duplex with Marley and Bear so each couple had a place to stay when they popped down for a visit. Acacia and I found a cute Hemingway inspired home within walking distance to our inlet that we instantly fell in love with.

Walking into that house, knowing we'd be bringing home our child to raise in roughly eight months, centered me in a way I never expected to feel. Some days, it felt like a dream. I didn't think Acacia and I would ever get to the point where we were friends, let alone lovers. But I would spend every day showing her how earnestly I loved her.

For those who have read me before, you know that I use my mea culpa to admit/acknowledge/accept all of the shit that I took serious creative license on in my book. As a reminder this Mea Culpa is a literal last minute brain dump thrown into the back of the book just before I hit publish—so there's probably going to be typos. No one sees this but me. Oh.. and probably swearing because by the time I get to this part the four letter kind of words are pretty much all that's left.

So if you've been reading me straight through it's been a while since you've had a published book from me. (I think Mile High Monarch). Anyhow for me it seems like I haven't stopped writing since then, but they're all stories going into anthologies so "you" won't see them for a while.

**2026 Update*

Im just going to leave all the other ones in here like a running diary. So originally this was part of a series called The Man of the Month and is set in Candy Cane Key. Each author in the series had a month - mine was July- and it was a whole thing. Regardless I'm not part of that group anymore—when my mom died I got quietly exited from a lot of groups so if you want to read more about Candy Cane key OUTSIDE of this book you can search them on Amazon. I think unfortunately this book the digital version is still connected to the world so you can find the rest of that series. But I am not writing anything else in that world.

If I end up doing a follow up book with Edwin and Acacia it would be more focused in my own ecosystem and less concern with accuracy across the year's worth of books. Just an FYI.

****2024 Updated Mea Culpa *****

I say that because it seems strange to not be able to reference those books that won't come out until next year when discussing this one. First I guess I should address the elephant in the room as to why my release got pushed back. I know it was supposed to come out about three weeks ago. My mom *was* sick at the time of this publishing. I had to drop everything to fly to Chicago and the last thing I was thinking about while at home was making sure I could get my manuscript to my proof reader, get it formatted, put up for ARCs etc etc while dealing with everything going on back at home. Life happens, and my publishing schedule had to adjust. As you all know I don't write full time, I still juggle a regular 9-5 and cobble together stories in gasps of time between life, work, family and motivation. Anyhow the book is out YAY and there's a lot of shorter/anthology type stories coming down the pike so you'll see I haven't been slacking off since February haha.

Since this book, my mom suddenly and unexpectedly passed away in October of 2023. It has been the hardest and most stressful year I've ever had to push through. I was so deep in the denizen of grief and the never ending needs of having to close out the estate for someone who died without anything prepared. I was drowning for the longest time and honestly feared I would never find my way back up.

But, as of September 2023, almost nearing the one year anniversary of her passing, I'm slowly finding my way back to land on shaky legs battle weary, but I think, finally ready to dip my toes back into the worlds I love.

I had numerous books that I had to cancel preorders on and currently sit barely started or halfway finished in my drafts. One day, hopefully soon, I'll be able to get back to them and deliver on all the publishing promises I made to everyone That's why in the "Willow's Worlds" you'll see a lot of "coming soon" without specific dates. Because honestly right now I still don't know when I'll be able to fall back into writing like I used to. I'm trying to be gentle on myself and not have any expectations. 😅

On to the Mea Culpas!

1. This book was written in 2023. As of right now Hemingway is 124 not 125 but I liked the 125 because it fit better... I feel like everyone would put more meaning behind those five year markers so Acacia would be more upset at a 120 more than a 119 for "the incident" So... Mea Culpa. For anyone who is a Hemingway expert or looked it up, yes I fudged his timeline.

2. On the topic of Hemingway, I only know enough about Hemingway to me sound like I know what I'm talking about. Most of the shit I put in here about Hemingway was #Siroti. Also, I'm only going off what has been written about his drinking and womanizing. I have no idea how much of it is actually true.

3. My apologies to the Hemingway family. I'm sure that they are all lovely and generous people who would graciously laugh at an "incident" where someone shows them their tits and then pukes over the side of a boat. I bet they wouldn't hold it against the host of the event, since it would be out of their control.

4. I know shit all about pirates and especially female pirates. Though there was this pirate show on Showtime for a while back in like the late 2000s or mid 2010s—IDK time has become fuzzy now that Im 40. But I watched the shit out of that pirate show. It was the first time I think I'd ever seen a show on TV where there was full male frontal and DAMN 👀 the main pirate in that show had quite the "mast" 💯. Anyhow, the information I shared about those two female pirates whose names Ive already forgotten and I don't want to go searching through my manuscript were based on academic articles I saw on JSTOR (which is an academic site where professors post papers and well if you're in school you have to search it obsessively for peer reviewed articles on whatever the hell you're researching.)

5. Speaking of academia... those in academia, please don't come for me for misrepresenting the process of becoming a full professor. I know like a nose hairs worth of information about universities. Other than being around and witnessing the insular politics I never actually had to try to become a full professor so Mea Culpa, seriously.

5a. Also I'm sorry to anyone who attended the University of Florida. Originally I was going to use FSU because I'd always heard that FSU was a huge party school. But even then—I feel like everyone labels every school as a huge party school. (Except Iowa, we know it's true for them. 🥴). Anyway based on #Siroti University of Florida is apparently considered the bigger party school of the two. Also, it actually had history classes on Pirates and I didn't see anything like that at FSU.

5b. I know absolutely nothing about Maritime history. I just needed something that made sense for someone who worked a boat and lived in Florida and of course, Pirates because why not hahah

6. Did anyone catch the Mrs Soames reference? That would be from another literary great, who wrote a little play called *Our Town by* Thornton Wilder. Fun fact I was Mrs Soames in my high school version. I went to an all girls school and we had literally no budgets for our plays. So we didn't have the fancy sets and the practically broadway esque budgets to make our productions top notch.

So our version of Our Town was done Theater in the Round Style. No sets. Just us, only costumes and a spotlight, —which made us have to really *act* without depending on props or anything else that makes acting easier.

Anyhow our narrator was played by a woman, because all girls school - her name was Sarah and she did an amazing job. SO much so that when my college did Our Town my freshman year, I auditioned for the role of the narrator. I got a standing ovation from the people at the audition and I was absolutely *crushed* when they told me they weren't casting a female in that role that it was written as a man and so they were casting it as a man. They offered me some stupid assed role as like "woman in cemetery number two" I gave them the double finger and never auditioned for another play at in college again.

7. If you read the MOTM in order you're more than likely just coming off Come to Papa— Matilda Martel's book. I intentionally use the phrase more than once in my book and

mention Felix and Harlow as a nod to her and her story. (Also if you've read *my* book **Flirt Like a Champ** my Harlow and her Harlow are not the same people... we just both have great taste in naming characters 😉). They were sort of aligned. Book nerds.academics, Hemingway. She and I are pretty similar in our neediness for literary things. And when we signed up for holidays for this years MOTM I practically humped the calendar laying claim to Hemingway Day. I don't know if she wanted it too... but given she's right before me in June maybe she did 😬 But so that's why I have Edwin say "Come to Papa"

If you know your Hemingway you might know that he was referred to as Papa. Which was sort of why I had Edwin say it.

If this is the first book you're read from me and you're curious about the Asher/Marley sub plot: Asher and Marley's mom don't have a story. It was something I threw in as an aside in Marley's story: Screwg'd — it continued in her and Bear's Wedding Story: Independence Bae, and continued even further in Witch Please. That little plot point has been hanging out there for so damn long that when I finally saw MOTM was going to be based in the Keys I thought now is my chance to finally close that loop. So if you want to learn about Marley, Bear, and that whole world, those would be the books to start with. Also, if you want to hear about that reunion from Marley's perspective, keep scrolling I've added it as a bonus scene. It's a rough that I wrote AFTER this was edited and proofed so its got my eyes on it, and ProWritingAid.. so please don't come at me for nitpicky stuff please and thank you.

As you'll see — my characters all kind of pop in and out of each others books, so through those you'll meet other characters and you can follow any number of branches about other people. They (Marley & Ted/Bear) also briefly get mentioned in Felicity's Sister's book: Date & Switch and then in Felicity & Klaus' book: Rental Clause

8. If you're reading the Christmas in July from MOTM books alongside the regular MOTM Books and you're like no one else mentions this Tropical Storm, Willow. I'm not part of the xmas in July group and I've had a storm planned in mine since I put up my blurb—so

9. Yes I put yet another person/group of people at Oxford. IDK why. It just seemed to make sense if Acacia's mom was from Spain that if she were a high achiever, Oxford would be in her sights. I have to do the math and see if Acacia would have been there at the same time as any of my other Oxonians. I feel like she might overlap with Sebastian, Imogen and Phoebe. Perhaps at some point there will be some quirky kismety way to bring them all together.

Speaking of kismety things... I don't think I had a single sign from the universe with this book. It could be because there is such a hurricane of life happening right now that I wasn't as attuned to or dialed in as I usually am. IDK. Now I'm a little bit bummed that there's nothing to offer up.

10. I know nothing about hurricanes. I apologize to any Floridian that is like Willow you trippin. Mea Culpa. My only experience with hurricanes and tropical storms are from my in-laws who live in Port Charlotte. And when there was literally a hurricane barreling down on them they were like "meh—it probably will just be a little rain and maybe some mud in our lanai" and my husband and I were like THE EYE IS LITERALLY PROJECTED TO PASS RIGHT OVER YOUR HOUSE and they were all . We all grew up in the midwest. We had tornados and that was it. Maybe I over-

blow the tropical storm but I figured its similar to a really bad thunderstorm that has tornado like winds without the tornado.

11. Six-Toed Joe, a black and white, six toed kitty with a black mustache that makes him look like a Mario, is actually a real cat. But his name isn't Six-Toed Joe and he doesn't live in the Florida Keys. His name is actually Mario, and he belongs to my friend Author Melissa Huie and he is SO cute. So... sorry not sorry for putting her cute little kitty, six toes and all in my story.

12. Also, yes I did in fact drop yet another Gilmore Girls reference into a book. :) They will never get old for me. Haha. I recently read somewhere that when you are stressed out that you return to comfort shows because you know what is going to happen in them and therefore you don't have anxiety over the outcome of each episode. Gilmore Girls has always been that show for me. My husband has actually gotten to the point that when he comes home from work snd sees me watching an episode of Gilmore Girls he's like "Oh shit what happened?" I will always be Team Logan haha and the more I read about Amy Sherman Paladino the more disappointed I am, but Gilmore Girls will never not be my favorite show.

I dedicated this book to my friend, fellow author M.A. Foster. She and I are sprinting partners. In that we message one another on weekends and say "hey are you writing" and then we set a timer for usually thirty minutes and write. If it wasn't for her, this book legitimately wouldn't have gotten finished. She also incidentally lives in Florida. While I'm writing this book she's writing a college football book so I'd be like "How soon would people start evacuating for a tropical storm" and she'd be like "Where would a tight end place in the draft." It was a blissful partnership.

Alright, I think that is it for me. Keep turning for a piece from Marley and some of the rest of what I've been doing.

As always, thank you so much to each of you for supporting my dreams. There is nothing I love more than coming and playing make believe in worlds of my choosing. (And hearing from readers always gives me a boost—legit) Especially the ones who mention how much you love my Mea Culpas hahaha

Writing has always been my solace and my escape, and I am eternally grateful that you sit down somewhere around the world, take hold of my hand, and allow me to show you what I've created. Thank you. From the very bottom of my heart.

As aways Andi Lynne and the Unicorn Tribe there is no one I am more grateful to than each of you. ILY infinity. xox

Marley Meets Asher

Marley

Ever since the day Ted gifted me the information his private investigator tracked down; I've felt like I'm in a never ending game of Marco/Polo. We get close to the answer, only to have to pivot and chase down another rabbit hole. I try not to get too upset with my mom. She was even younger than me when she found out she was going to be a mom. And I know that must have been scary. Especially doing it on your own.

I'd never know why she didn't just go back to Dartmouth and talk to Dr. Asher Krane about her situation. Or called, sent a letter, anything in the thirty years I'd been alive to let him know about me. After all the months of searching for him, he finally sat across from me. Total shock. Abject terror. Confusion. Hurt. Distrust. Many emotions played across his face and instead of being angry with him, I felt myself getting pretty pissed at my mom.

"I know. It's a pretty big shock." I told him. "I'm sorry to spring it on you in the middle of this big event." I signaled to the melee around us as people set up tables and pulled chairs from the back of the pub.

"Marley, you don't owe anyone an apology." Ted took my hand and squeezed.

He was my rock. I don't know what I'd do without him. Given he was a foster kid himself, he'd always been insistent that we pursue finding as much as we could about my birth father. So I had closure. Answers to any questions I may have had. And now that we had Tillie and Nick, the desire for them to have at least one grandparent spurred us even harder to look for Asher.

"No, of course not. Your husband is correct, Marley. You do not owe me any assurances. I fear I am the one who owes you a lifetime of explanations. My silence is not because of you. You simply caught me off guard."

While we sat in a corner booth and chatted, I took an inventory of his likenesses and tried to find anything that tied my DNA to his. While tall, he was thicker than my mom and me. She and I were both pretty petite. I had my mom's blue eyes. Asher's were dark brown. The deeper set of his eyes didn't align with mine, nor did his aristocratic nose or his narrow lips. Maybe we were wrong all along. And while she had a crush on Asher or loved him, a college boyfriend or someone else was the one who actually knocked her up.

"Do you think it's possible?" I asked. "That you could be my dad? I mean, the dates lineup, but I'm looking at you trying to find even the slightest similarities and I'm coming up empty."

I didn't want to go through this again. We'd been on the hunt since our wedding day. If Asher wasn't my dad, I didn't think I had the emotional strength to ride this roller coaster again.

Asher looked over his shoulder at all the bustle surrounding us.

"Would the two of you like to come back to my home? I'm just around the corner. We could take my golf cart if you'd like."

Ted looked over at me and shrugged. It seemed silly to deny an invite to his house. Especially if he was, in fact, my dad.

Candy Cane Key was a sweet little town. There was no way you could keep a secret in a town as small as that. It seemed like everyone was in each other's business.

"I hope it doesn't rain." He pointed toward the clouds that seemed to approach the coast on a mission.

Asher jingled the keys in his pocket, unlocking the door to a sweet robin's egg blue A-frame with a cobblestone path lined with magnolia trees. I don't know if I had an expectation of what my dad's house would look like— whomever my dad ended up being—I don't know if Asher's home would have ever been in any of my wildest imaginations.

Despite the beachy vibe of the street and the typical Florida Keys appearance of his neighborhood, his inside screamed old time Downton Abby library. I half expected a butler to appear and take my coat. I'd never seen so many bookshelves, let alone so many books in my life.

"I have some photos upstairs in my study." He pointed to the six steps that separated the first and second floors. "Please have a seat. I'll be right back."

Ted signaled for me to take one of the leather wingback

chairs. Rather than sit as well, he chose instead to work out our shared anxiety by pacing around the room. Every so often he'd stop and stare at some artifact that sat on a shelf, or a book on display.

"I wanted a simpler life when I retired here." Asher laughed to himself, pointing to his overflowing shelves and brick-a-brac that were scattered around. "But when push came to shove, there were too many things I just couldn't get rid of. So my quaint little home isn't nearly as minimalist as I'd hoped."

He took the chair opposite me and placed a large box on the table. This moment had been so long coming, and now that it was here? My body didn't know how to react. It thrilled me to get some answers, maybe some closure, and hopefully—if I was truly being honest—a path forward. But I needed to protect my stupid heart. It was already a trilling damn songbird, planning to expand the nest.

"I grew up in Vermont. It was me, my sister Cecily, and my brother Jonas." Asher pulled out pictures from the box and showed me old black and white photos of the three of them playing in the snow and running around a pine tree covered backyard.

"Look at this." I passed a picture of him and his sister to Ted.

"If not for the black and white—this could be Nick and Tillie."

Hearing Ted give voice to exactly what I'd been thinking brought a wave of tears. I'd spent the afternoon trying to figure out where Asher was in my genes. I'd seen nothing that even hinted at our being related. My kids though? Absolutely no doubt. Tillie had a sweet little button nose that turned up at the end. Through their infancy Ted and I had marveled at them morphing and growing and assumed that her and her brother's looks must have been from Ted's unknown family members. The three Krane kids all sported curly hair in one form of another. While my hair was wavy, I did not inherit the thick ringlets that they had.

"Your grandkids." I woke up my iPhone and showed Asher the wallpaper on my phone, which was set to our last holiday card photo. "They're two and a half. Tillie Joy and Nicholas Charles."

Asher took my phone and stared at it for a long, silent moment.

"I never thought—" his voice caught as he tried to finish his sentence. "My whole adult life, I mourned the loss of this. Not having any family. My brother has already passed and my sister and I don't get to see one another very often. And as you get to be my age, you think about your own mortality. Your legacy. What you've shared with the world. Despite leaving my mark at Dartmouth, I never got to experience this."

He handed my phone back to me. Something about looking him right in his wrinkled eyes that had me vibrating with empathy. Hope. He looked at me with hope in those eyes. As if seeing my family had him hoping that perhaps he too, could become part of us.

"They're a handful." Ted said, "Double the trouble. But I wouldn't change it for the world."

Asher pushed himself out of his chair, mumbling something about drinks and food. While he busied himself brewing a pot of coffee based on the smell, and assembling some cookies on a plate based on the sounds, Ted flipped through more of Asher's childhood photos. Occasionally he'd hold one up for me to see, as if to show me even more proof that we'd found our familial missing link.

"I know you want to know about your mom," Asher began as he passed out the coffee mugs. "I'm happy to tell you anything I can. But I also have to admit I'm a little nervous. I know from where you sit that it probably seems terribly wrong for me to have had any kind of relationship with someone thirty years my junior. But Joy was so incredibly intelligent I often forgot she was only eighteen.

"She came to campus in the summer." He looked out the front window of his house, lost in thought. "There was a summer theater workshop for all incoming freshmen who were considering pursuing theater as a major—which Joy was. The professors working the summer theater intensive were paired up with three of four students to work on monologues, group work, have them get acclimated to the quicker pace of college theater. And, of course, introduce them to the rich, complicated prose of Shakespeare. That was our bread and butter. Dartmouth's Shakespeare festival is world renown. There is an expectation that we deliver the highest theatrical standard. Our summer programs and degrees were highly competitive. I don't want to get too far into the details and embarrass you." He continued, "but being with Joy was addictive, intoxicating. She saw the word through fresh eyes, and having a woman who had never experienced more than the shy fumblings of a teenager—it was all I could think about, introducing her to the world of an adult sexual relationship. I guess the thrill of sneaking around made it even more salacious."

The words sat heavy and thick on my tongue. I desperately wanted to know. Needed to. But also I didn't want to give voice to the question I knew, in my bones, I already had the answer to.

My mom had to shoulder the burden of a mistake that took two people to make. Her whole life flew out the window the day that strip turned pink. Joy Jacobs morphed from an eighteen-year-old with a superhighway in front of her to an unmarried, pregnant teen with limited options in a small mountain town. She had been my sun and my moon. Every scratch and bruise, fear and worry, as well as every happiness, no matter how large or small, were rooted deep within her memories.

As a mom now myself, I struggled to wrap my head around how my mom did it. She was an exiled daughter, with no money and few skills, trying to make it on her own with barely enough money to afford the basics.

"Did you love her?"

The second Asher's eyebrows dropped, and the reflective smile faltered, I knew. I'd always known. Otherwise, he would have gone after her. Tried to find her. Or at the bare minimum written to her and asked after why she'd left college.

"I don't want to cause you anymore hurt than you've already suffered, Marley."

At least he had the decency to be honest.

"I was and probably still am a pretty egotistical man. I loved how your mom made me feel. Young, desired, intellectually superior. The way she looked at me, it was as if I were personally responsible for creating the solar system, and it was a heady and addictive thing. I took advantage of a young woman who was barely starting out in the world, and as much as I loved the way I felt around her, it wasn't right."

I felt Ted's agitation from across the room. He pressed

out of his seat on the couch, the stormy look in his eyes and the viscous set of mouth was practically a billboard screaming his upset into the room.

"Marley, I think you've gotten what you came for. Let's head back to the hotel and see if we can get our flights adjusted. It's clear there's nothing in this town for you."

Asher stood as well, hands up in surrender, approaching Ted as if he were a wounded, rabid animal.

"Please." Asher said, extending his hand toward Ted. In that moment, I realized how frail Asher was, despite his dignified presence. If he had been in his forties when my mom and he were involved, he'd easily be somewhere in his seventies.

"Please stay. I'm at the age where I'm too old for artifice. I don't want to build a relationship with a daughter I just learned I had, with a false idea of who her mom and I were. Because eventually the truth would surface."

Ted looked at me and suddenly, despite being able to decide and stand on my own two feet for years, I didn't know what to do. It was clear Ted wanted to leave, and I wanted to leave with him. It was evident he needed to be soothed. There was some kind of malaise twisting the face that seemed to always be filled with laughter and light.

But I also needed to hear it all. I came to Candy Cane Key for information, and I needed all of it. To suck it dry like a vampire.

"I'm sorry, Marley." Ted collected me against his side and pressed his mouth to my earlobe. "I just wanted to give you something I'll never get."

He didn't need to apologize. I didn't even want an apology from him. He spent every hour of each day ensuring that me and the kids felt the warmth of his love and the soft hold of his protection. I fell more in love with him every day we spent together. And I knew, regardless of the decision to stay or go, he'd support me.

"It's okay, Ted." I led him to the sofa so we could sit side by side. "I'd like to hear about Asher's life. Even if it didn't involve mom."

Asher seemed surprised. As if he'd expected me to walk out as much as Ted wanted me to do just that. I wanted to do this for my mom as much as I wanted the information for myself. Just in case, at some point in her life, she'd wondered what if. I'd get that answered for her. And perhaps wherever she was, she'd hear us talking too.

"I didn't know about you, Marley. Your mom and I had our dalliance throughout the fall semester. We had our fall festival, A Midsummer's Night's Dream and Joy was just otherworldly. She had such a natural talent for the stage. When a spotlight was on your mom, and she looked out into the audience, it was magnetic. Absolutely magical."

I saw it. Asher had feelings for my mom, even if they never categorized them as love. It was in the way his lip curled into a bittersweet smile, and his eyes got glossy and stared off as if watching her in his mind's eye. His mouth even moved to words only he could hear.

"Then our classes finished up for the semester, your mom went back home for winter break, and I never saw her again."

"You didn't think to call her? Or write? Something? Didn't you wonder what happened to her?" I asked. "If the two of you had this hot and heavy thing going on, wouldn't you have at least cared enough about her to want to know if she was okay? Were you not even the slightest bit concerned that she may have died on the way home from school? Or something happened to her? I just can't imagine having feelings for someone…"

I pointed at Ted, trying to show that in my head I would have never in a million years done something like that to him. Ted wrapped my hand in his gigantic one, bringing it to his mouth. The moment his lips whispered across my pulse point; my anxiety abated to a low simmer.

"Help me understand, Asher. You must have cared for my mother in some facet to have had unprotected sex with her."

"I cared for her very much, Marley. And sometimes birth control ends up not working." Asher shrugged sheepishly. "But our relationship was unconventional and inappropriate if we're being totally honest. After she left, I assumed maybe her parents found out about us, or maybe she'd gone home and met a boy her own age and transferred out to get a fresh start.

"I reasoned it was probably better that it ended that way. And, as sad as I was to see her leave so abruptly, in my heart I wished her well and always hoped she'd had the best life."

I swiped at a tickle on my cheek and realized I'd started crying. Asher noticed as well and passed me a hanky from his pocket. He must have seen the question on my face because he laughed, shaking it a bit, and assuring me it was unused.

"My mother always told me to put two hankies in my pocket. One for me, and one to offer a stranger."

It even had his initials embroidered into it.

"Did you ever get married?" I asked him, trying to clean my face while trying to salvage my eye makeup.

He shook his head, studying his hands.

"I'm not very likeable, I'm afraid." He admitted. "I'm moody. A little self-absorbed. I have a hard time balancing my focus. My career...my vanity...had me desperate to chase after every accolade and acclaim. There have been some lovely companions in my life, but they all learned eventually that I'm not worth the effort."

Something about his matter-of-fact appraisal broke me. I wanted to show him how easy loving someone could be. To teach him what Ted had shown me since the first time I met him back at the costume rental shop in North Pole. Loving is as simple as breathing when someone loves you.

"I think that the reason I discovered mom's dress right before my wedding is because mom knew I was at a place to accept that life and love are messy and complicated. And she waited until we were past the insanity of learning how to manage our lives with twins before she put me in a place to come and see you.

"Being a mom to those two," I signaled to the picture on my cell phone again, "showed me just how easy it is to love someone. And maybe that's the lesson mom wanted me to learn before I came and found you. Because Tillie and Nick are the easiest people to fall in love with. And I would assume it's the same way with any parent."

"I didn't know you existed before an hour ago, and already I don't want you to leave, Marley. There are so many things I want to learn about you. Past the basic things like where you went to college and what you do for a living, but what fills your heart with joy? What is your passion? Were you in school plays? Do you act? Love books? Academia?"

Each question felt like a pelt of ice against a glass window. Asher seemed so excited to see the places where his

DNA pumped through my veins. And the last thing I wanted was to disappointment him with how boring I was.

"I followed my mom to Dartmouth." I began. "I think even though at that point I didn't know who you were, I thought somehow maybe I'd stumble into someone with bright blue eyes and curly hair and suddenly I'd find my dad. But mom got diagnosed with M.S. right before I started college, and by the end of my freshman year, she needed my help full time."

Ted's arm wrapped protectively around my shoulder again. He pressed his lips against my forehead before picking up the conversation with Asher.

"Marley has incredibly artistic talent. And she loves Christmas. She's combined those two things and runs an online boutique for custom holiday decorations. Marley is modest to the nth degree, so she'd never brag about how successful it is. But between raising our two kids and running a successful business, I'm constantly in awe of her."

Asher's lip quirked in a half smile. He caught me looking at him and nodded. As if to say I'd found a good one. He wasn't wrong. I'd found the best one.

"And where do the two of you call home?" Asher asked again.

"Chicago." Ted and I said nearly at the same time. "But I still own the bed-and-breakfast that belonged to mom. One of our best friends runs a chain of hotels and handles the business end of things as well as keeping up our family residence. But it's been forever since we've been to North Pole."

"North Pole is fairly close to Dartmouth, right? Perhaps this fall you and I could pay a visit to my old haunt and I can introduce you to Dr. Doyle, who now runs the Shakespeare

Festival. You can see what it was like when your mom did A Midsummer's Night's Dream."

I realized he didn't know the whole crazy story that got us to this point. With a deep breath and a grounding sip from my cooling coffee, I regaled him with the entire story.

"We've already met Sebastian and Imogen." I smiled, trying to keep from giggling. "They are a sort of honorary auntie and uncle to the kids. We went to the festival the year after you'd retired, which was Sebastian's first. I was eight months pregnant and positively miserable. But I wanted to meet you because I thought I couldn't be a good mom if I didn't know who I was. And I felt like there was a huge piece of me missing because I only knew half of me.

"Ted and I trekked out to Dartmouth and wouldn't you know it? The babies decided they wanted to be born that very weekend. We make it a point now to return to the festival every year with the kids. Sebastian and Imogen are married now. They split their time between Dartmouth and Oxford, and share the title of co-chair for the literary festival."

Asher threw his head back and laughed a rich belly laugh. One that lightened all of his features and took at least a decade from his face. Just witnessing the totally unexpected delight had me joining in, even though I did not know what he was laughing at.

"That is a pairing I never would have expected." He wiped at the tears streaming from his eyes. "They are as different as tomato paste and habanero salsa."

I pointed at Ted. Mr. Rock and Roll, covered in a blanket of tattoos from head to toe. I knew looked strange to others. But there was no one in the world better for me than him.

"Point taken." Asher held up his hands in defeat. "And

the two of you seem genuinely happy. It's nice to see. Now, I know this is brand new—what we have. But maybe you'd let me join you this fall? I'd love to show you around campus and really give you some background on the place."

He sounded so vulnerably hopeful. And it felt so right. Like I'd always known that in my coming here, this is exactly what it would lead to. A piece of family for me and Ted and the kids.

"When we got married, Ted's boss, Ivy, made me my wedding gown. She told me that her deceased mother believed in the universe's magic and felt like she had crossed paths with us just when we were getting married because she had the talent and the means to create a wedding dress that looked just like the one my mom wore for A Midsummer's Nights Dream. And I believe in that same magic, Asher. Otherwise, why would I have had Ivy there for my wedding, that tied to Dartmouth, where my babies unexpectedly arrived and now we visit each year, where you also taught. I truly think this is what mom wanted for me, Asher."

"And is it what you want?" He asked. "Because the moment you told me you were my child, I suddenly feel this ache, right here."

He gestured to the pocket of his shirt. He took hold of the fabric and rest his hand there while looking toward me. I felt it too. Call it a connection. Or even the recognition that this man was, in fact, my father. But whatever the feeling was, it felt perfect. Like it had been there all along.

"Welcome to fatherhood." Ted raised his coffee cup toward Asher, an entertained smirk on his face.

"Fatherhood." Asher repeated, his voice filled with wonder.

"I think we should try." I told him honestly. "It's going to be weird for a while."

"Do I have stories about some weird situations!" Asher wiped at his mouth, covering his smile. "I have to say that suddenly finding out I have a daughter, and she has a husband and two children, I suddenly have hope again. And I promise you Marley, I will try my darndest every single day to be worth of the title as your dad."

"Don't forget the title of Grandpa," Ted added in. "The kids will finally have a grandparent. And that will be a title you'll need to earn. Because we've mourned the fact that they had no one since the day we found out Marley was pregnant. And anyone who gets the honor of being in our kids' lives has to earn a place."

"I'd expect nothing less, Ted." Asher extended his hand, shaking on the promise.

"I'm a grandpa." Asher announced, his voice choked with emotion. "I'll finally be able to eat at the tea shop and the country club or the donut shop with the rest of the septuagenarians who whip out their phones and wallets and brag over their kids and grandkids."

I gobbled up his excited delight. Imagining all the years that stretched in front of us. We could have him at our house for the holidays, or even come and visit Candy Cane Key. We could travel together on our annual trip to Dartmouth. The one time we would know that we would see one another.

I sent a sentence of gratitude up to my mom. The three of us sat in genial silence for a moment. His old mantle clock tick-ticked, the wind outside rattled the windows, but I didn't want to leave and disrupt the feeling of having a place, with a person, who eventually would become as significant in my life as Ted and the kids.

It was a wonderful realization. My family was about to grow by one significant human being. And it was all thanks to Ted.

"How long are the two of you in town?" Asher broke me from my musings.

"We fly out the day after tomorrow."

"You are in luck then!" He raised his finger, his face filling with pride and excitement. "Tomorrow is a very important day both to me and to Candy Cane Key. It's Ernest Hemingway's one hundred and twenty-fifth birthday, and we're about to have an amazing celebration. I'd love for you to be my guests at the party. I'm afraid I was supposed to be helping them set up, but this was far more pressing. However, my good friend Acacia, the proprietor of Temperance, she's a spitfire. One of the smartest women I've ever met. And we are about to herald in Mr. Hemingway's one hundred and twenty-fifth year with a bang!"

We all stood, and he walked us to the door as he chattered on about the finer details of the party, including the menu, which was full of puns that flew clear over my head.

"And for the first time in my life, I get to introduce my guest as a member of my family. My daughter."

His arm clasped my shoulder. I felt it. The way he held himself back. His respectful hold on my elbow as he opened my door. The warm, pride filled smile as we walked over the threshold.

"Thank you." I pulled him into a hug, and the surprised gasp and pleased mmm told me my instinct was spot on. "I'm so glad that we took a chance and flew down here, Asher. Thank you for being so welcoming."

"I am going to be the very best late-to-the-game father, Marley. I promise. You have me, heart and soul."

I didn't doubt it. Not for a second. Being with him, seeing his pictures and hearing his stories. I knew I needed more. I wanted it all. To gluttonously feast on any tidbit, he'd provide me. Because finally, after over thirty years of wondering who he was, I knew who my dad was—warts and all—and I couldn't wait to get to know him even more.

Felicity

The last place I wanted to be for Christmas was home. I knew when my twin sister, Sera, called me and begged me to come home that it could only mean one thing. That her perfect boyfriend she met *because of me* turned out to be *the* one.

That's why she wanted everyone home spending Christmas with the family. So Bryce could finally meet me, the twin, in person. Except I was still an open wound, reeling from my own *Mr. The One* deciding he wanted to tap out so he could *tap* our neighbor in 4E.

With the whole family home, there was no way in hell I was spending the week on the couch. With Sera and *Mr. The One* sleeping in our former shared bedroom, the lifeline to my sanity was an AirBnB--the last one available in an entire twenty-mile radius.

Klaus

This year could slip on a patch of ice and land on a pile of legos. First, some chump stole my identity, then the pipes in my condo burst. Given it was the week of Christmas, there was no room at any inn, stable, or motel. Not that I could even stay if there was a vacancy since I had no credit to my name until all this identity thief b.s. sorted itself out. I would rather sleep in the snow than share my brother's house with his four kids--so I gladly jump at his wife's suggestion I stay at our rental property. It was the perfect solution except for one minor problem--a curvy little firecracker with a rental confirmation dangling from her holiday-themed manicured hand.

When a blizzard disrupts their holiday plans, the pair will soon learn they're getting much more than they bargained for!

Meet Marley and Bear!

DJ Ted "Bear" Tucker is officially done with Christmas. If he has to play *All I Want for Christmas Is You* and someone's getting impaled with a candy cane. Unfortunately, the holidays are his job, and they're about to get a whole lot worse.

Marley Jacobs needs something to go right. Instead, she's been crowned the town's Holiday Scrooge, publicly humiliated on the local radio station, and paired with the grumpiest DJ in North Pole as her so-called "magic maker." In her opinion, Ted Tucker is one holiday elf who should be permanently shelved.

What starts as mutual annoyance quickly turns into stolen glances, sizzling tension, and a connection neither of them planned for. But when the season puts their hearts on the line, Teddy and Marley will have to decide if they're enemies by circumstance...or soulmates in disguise.

Because when love and the holidays collide, someone always ends up **Screwg'd**.

Heir Agreement: The Hawthorne Brothers

None of the Above (Ellis & Rowan)

Good on Paper (Whit & Tennie)

No Comment (Keats & …)

Terms & Conditions (Dash & …)

Love on the Air Series

Screwg'd (Bear & Marley)

Bed of Roses (Raven & Penn)

Independence Bae (Bear & Marley, Raven & Penn and some old friends from Dirty Little Secret & Secrets of the Heart)

The Miller Sisters (Love on the Air Spinoff)

Date & Switch (Sera Miller & Bryce Ellis (Penn's Brother)

Rental Clause (Felicity Miller & Klaus Baer)

Under a Starlit Sky (Date & Switch Spin Off) – Appeared in Christmas Anthology will release soon

Enemies in Ernest (Acacia & Edwin (Klaus' Cousin)

Salve (Rex Miller & Regina Cole - Felicity & Sera's brother) Coming soon!

The Murray Brothers

Thirst Trap (Beckett & Lane)

Flirt Like a Champ (Cash Murray & Harlow Prince)

Secret Santa (Priscilla King & Presley Murray)

Redhead in Bed (Harris Murray and Lorelei Donnegan)

King of the Cul De Sac -*Murray Brothers Spin Off*- (Lennox Shaw & Jesse King) Harlow's Sister & Priscilla's Brother

The Barren Hill Series

Beard on Tap (Finn & Gemini)

Codename: Dustoff (Emmett & Amelia)

Whiskey Business - *A Barren Hill Spinoff*- (Jasper & Remle)

A Whole New World (*A Whiskey Business Spinoff*, Coming Eventually)

The Jones Brothers (Coming Soon!)

Capivate Me (Sterling Cooper Jones)

Titillate Me   (Sullivan Carter Jones)

Extracurricular Academics

Booking Dr. Wrong (Dr. Patrick Ryan & Tabitha Spence)

Witch Please (Dr. Sebastian Doyle & Dr. Imogen Pilar)

Missed Connections (Dr. Phoebe Wagner & Anders Larochette)

The Royals - An Extracurricular Academics Spin Off

Mile High Monarch (A Missed Connections Spin Off)

The Expireship (A Mile High Monarch Spin Off) Coming Soon!

Deck Pic (Sawyer & Wren)

The Power of Two (Soon)

Romantic Suspense

I Will Always Find You & Found (The Jefe Duet)

Contemporary New Adult

Dirty Little Secret

Secrets of the Heart

THE MURRAY BROTHERS SERIES
The Miller Sisters
BARREN HILL SERIES
LOVE IN THE AIR SERIES
EXTRA CURRICULAR ACADEMICS
WILLOW SANDERS
SCAN ME / SCAN ME / SCAN ME / SCAN ME / SCAN ME / SCAN ME / SCAN ME / SCAN ME